To Andrea Colvin,
whose superpower is making books
the best they can be

ABOUT THIS BOOK

The illustrations for this book were created digitally. This book was edited by Andrea Colvin and designed by Ann Dwyer, with art direction by Megan McLaughlin. The production was supervised by Erica Huang, and the production editor was Lindsay Walter-Greaney. The text was set in Skippy Sharp and Eliot Text.

Copyright © 2025 by Mark Crilley

Torn paper, Sticky note, shiny star stickers, green construction paper, yellow paper ripped, eraser, paper scraps, and torn paper with tape copyright © various contributors at Shutterstock.com

Cover illustration copyright © 2025 by Mark Crilley. Cover design by Ann Dwyer.

Cover copyright © 2025 by Hachette Book Group, Inc.

Little, Brown and Company
Hachette Book Group
1290 Avenue of the Americas, New York, NY 10104
Visit us at LBYR.com

First Edition: July 2025

Little, Brown and Company is a division of Hachette Book Group, Inc.
The Little, Brown name and logo are registered trademarks of Hachette Book Group, Inc.

The publisher is not responsible for websites (or their content) that are not owned by the publisher.

Little, Brown and Company books may be purchased in bulk for business, educational, or promotional use. For information, please contact your local bookseller or the Hachette Book Group Special Markets Department at special.markets@hbgusa.com.

Library of Congress Cataloging-in-Publication Data
Names: Crilley, Mark, author, illustrator.
Title: The Mighty Onion and Guinea Pig Girl / Mark Crilley.
Description: First edition. | New York : Little, Brown and Company, 2025. | Audience term: Preteens | Audience: Ages 8–12. | Summary: "Pam and Eliot must navigate the ups and downs of creating comics for their local newspaper, just as their careers start to take off in different directions."
—Provided by publisher.
Identifiers: LCCN 2024031963 | ISBN 9780316490542 (hardcover) | ISBN 9780316579407 (ebook)
Subjects: CYAC: Cartoonists—Fiction. | Cooperativeness—Fiction. | Friendship—Fiction. | LCGFT: Diary fiction.
Classification: LCC PZ7.C869275 Mi 2025 | DDC [Fic]—dc23
LC record available at https://lccn.loc.gov/2024031963

ISBNs: 978-0-316-49054-2 (paper over board), 978-0-316-57940-7 (ebook), 978-0-316-57946-9 (ebook)

PRINTED IN DONGGUAN, CHINA

APS

10 9 8 7 6 5 4 3 2 1

THE MIGHTY ONION

and GUINEA PIG GIRL!

MARK CRILLEY

L B

LITTLE, BROWN AND COMPANY
NEW YORK   BOSTON

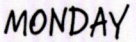
MONDAY

TODAY MELANIE AND I WENT TO THE BUBBLE TEA PLACE AFTER SCHOOL. I GOT SO ANGRY AT THE LADY WHO RUNS THE PLACE. SHE ALWAYS GOES: "YOU TWO SIT IN THE BACK ROOM. YOU'RE TOO LOUD AND IT BOTHERS THE CUSTOMERS." WE WERE LIKE:

LOYALTY CARD

THE LOOK ON HER FACE! SHE'S LUCKY SHE'S THE ONLY PERSON IN TOWN WHO MAKES A GOOD TARO-LYCHEE WITH EXTRA BUBBLES, 'CAUSE OTHERWISE THERE'S NO WAY WE'D STILL BE GOING THERE.

ANYWAY, MELANIE'S ALL EXCITED ABOUT SOMETHING SHE WANTS TO BAKE THIS WEEKEND.

SHE GOT THE IDEA FROM A VIDEO SHE SAW ONLINE, WHERE THIS GUY MADE COOKIES IN THE SHAPE OF EVERY PERSON HE HATES, AND THEN HE ATE ALL THEIR HEADS, ONE AT A TIME. IT'S SUPPOSED TO BE A REALLY GREAT STRESS RELIEVER.

MRS. GARCIA FOUND ME IN THE CAFETERIA TODAY AND ASKED IF I COULD DO A BIG DRAWING FOR HER OF A HAPPY SMILING TACO THAT'S DOING TWO THUMBS-UP AND SAYING "DELICIOSO!" MY FIRST THOUGHT WAS, "DUDE, NO WAY A LIVING TACO IS GONNA BE ENCOURAGING PEOPLE TO EAT TACOS." BUT I WENT AHEAD AND DID IT.

TUESDAY

TODAY IN CLASS, MRS. MACONIE SAID SHE TALKED TO HER FRIEND AT THE PIFFLING BUGLE, AND THAT THEY'VE DECIDED TO BEGIN RUNNING THE MIGHTY ONION STARTING NEXT MONTH. SO IT'S REAL NOW— IT'S REALLY HAPPENING!

I ASKED ELIOT IF HE WAS FINISHED MAKING CHANGES TO HIS SCRIPT FOR THE FIRST ISSUE, AND HE WAS LIKE:

RIGHT. WELL, IN THE INTEREST OF MAKING THIS ISSUE THE BEST IT CAN BE...

...I DECIDED TO JUNK THAT SCRIPT AND START ALL OVER AGAIN.

WHAT?!

I COULD'VE STRANGLED HIM. HOW AM I GONNA GET MY ART DONE WITHOUT A SCRIPT? I GAVE HIM UNTIL FRIDAY. IF HE'S NOT DONE BY THEN, WE'RE DOING "THIS MILK TASTES FUNNY TO ME."

With all the pressure I'm under right now, the last thing I needed was for Pam to come over to me today at school, freaking out about the script situation.

It's a good thing I was able to calm her down. I swear, half the job of working with an artist is being their therapist.

But yeah, it's crunch time. With the Piffling Bugle deadline just a couple weeks away, I need a breakthrough with this next script, and I need it, like, yesterday.

ISSUE 1: PLOT SUMMARY

The Mighty Onion, while attempting to rescue a different kitten from a different well, falls into a portal that sends him to an alternate dimension, where the composition of matter at the subatomic level causes him to grow an extremely unappealing mustache.

In this dimension, Guinea Pig Girl, owing to having been born in a different town, is Rabid Woodchuck Girl, which means she has enhanced powers but a really weird costume.

Since the Woodchuck Copter is in the shop for repairs, they must resort to public transportation to get to

~~UE~~ 1: PLOT SUMMARY

Guinea Pig Girl is shocked to find that the Mighty Onion has "gone rogue," joining forces with the Cuddler to smash the light bulb of the Guinea Pignal, making it impossible for Commissioner Groban to contact her when she is needed most.

Meanwhile, Dr. Hubris escapes from prison and, with the help of Granny McDoogle, executes a dastardly plan to sneak his mind-control serum into packages of Acme salt-and-vinegar potato c~~hi~~

The Mighty Onion, attempting to rescue stranded competitors in a dogsled race in the Arctic Circle, is accidentally frozen in ice and awakens in the year 2078, where he finds that Guinea Pig Girl is now a very old woman, retired from superhero work and living quietly in Idaho, where she devotes herself to cross-stitchi

NO!
NO!
NO!
NO!
NO!!

ELIOT, IT'S FRIDAY. WHERE'S THAT SCRIPT?

Just a few more finishing touches. Give me until Monday, OK?

YOU'RE OUT OF TIME, DUDE. JUST GIMME THE SCRIPT ALREADY. TODAY.

Pam. This thing is going to be read by THOUSANDS OF PEOPLE! It's gotta be perfect. And perfection takes time.

YOU KNOW WHAT TAKES TIME? DRAWING TAKES TIME! WAAAY MORE TIME THAN WRITING.

Will you calm down? You'll have it on Monday.

TELL ME THE BASIC PLOT. IF I KNOW THAT AT LEAST I CAN PREPARE A LITTLE.

Yeah, see, this one is really hard to summarize, Pam. Great literature is like that.

So what are your plans for the weekend?

IF I DON'T HAVE THAT SCRIPT FIRST THING MONDAY, I WILL **TEAR YOU LIMB FROM LIMB!!**

That's what I like to see, Pam: passion. Never lose that!

MONDAY!!!!

SUNDAY

YESTERDAY I WENT OVER TO MELANIE'S AND WE BAKED A TON OF COOKIES. SHE CHANGED HER MIND ABOUT THAT IDEA SHE HAD BEFORE, BECAUSE SHE SAID SHE WASN'T IN THE RIGHT MOOD FOR BITING OFF THE HEADS OF HER ENEMIES.

SO WE JUST DID A BUNCH OF RANDOM COOKIES LIKE WE USUALLY DO, WHERE THE GOAL IS TO COME UP WITH THE WEIRDEST IDEA POSSIBLE.

AFTER THAT WE WENT TO BOOKS-APLENTY FOR A WHILE, BUT MELANIE STARTED DANCING FOR SOME REASON, AND I COULDN'T STOP LAUGHING, AND THEY MADE US LEAVE. GOOD TIMES!

WHAT AM I GONNA DO?!

Pam needs the script by tomorrow, and I've got NOTHING! Every idea I come up with is like poop that has been rolled in garbage and then covered with poop.

It's the pressure of knowing my writing is gonna be in the Piffling Bugle. It's messing with my head.

It's all Mr. Budzinski's fault. He said I was good at writing, but what does HE know? HE'S AN ALGEBRA TEACHER!!

I'm starving. Maybe a snack will help.

OK, it's gonna sound like I made this up but I swear: I was a few bites in on this chocolate bar, and — BAM! — it hit me: the perfect plotline for issue 1.

The ideas were flowing so quickly I could barely write fast enough to keep up with them.

Next time this happens to me, I gotta learn my lesson...

...eat the candy bar as early in the process as possible!

And that's it. I've got a script I can hand off to Pam tomorrow. Which is good, because if I showed up at school empty-handed I'm pretty sure she would crush my head open with her bare hands.

<u>MONDAY</u>

ELIOT FINALLY GOT HIS SCRIPT DONE, SO NOW I'VE GOT, LIKE, FIVE DAYS TO FINISH ALL THIS ARTWORK. I SWEAR, IT'S A MIRACLE THERE ARE ANY SURVIVING WRITER-ARTIST TEAMS IN THE WORLD, BECAUSE EVERY OTHER DAY ELIOT DOES SOMETHING THAT MAKES ME WANT TO POKE HIM HARD IN THE EYES.

IN ALL HONESTY, IT'S KIND OF A WEIRD SCRIPT, AND I'M NOT SURE WHERE ELIOT IS GOING WITH ALL THIS. BUT THERE'S NO TIME TO GET STRESSED ABOUT THAT NOW. I'VE GOTTA GET THESE PAGES DONE!

THE MIGHTY ONION

ISSUE 1

Written by Eliot Quigly
Drawings by Pamela Jones

LATE ONE NIGHT, INSIDE THE METROVILLE MUSEUM OF PRICELESS ANTIQUITIES...

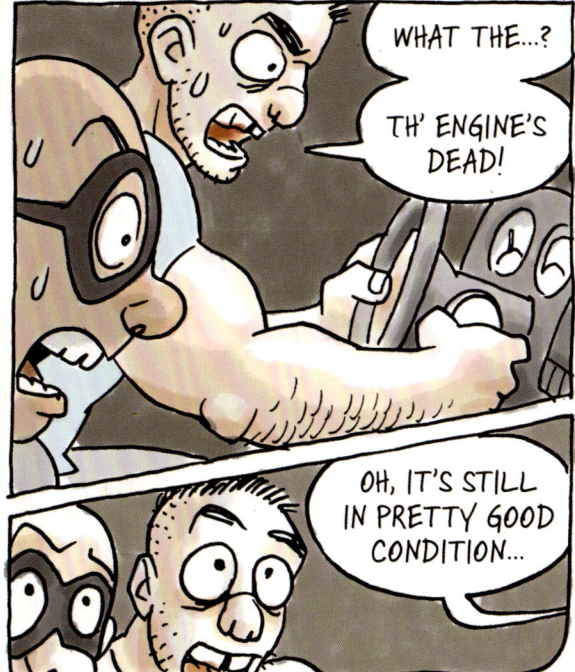

HEY THERE, ROCKY.

WHAT'S IN THE BAG?

SOON COMMISSIONER GROBAN AND HIS TEAM ARRIVE ON THE SCENE, AND OUR HEROES' WORK IS DONE.

MUSEUM OF

POLICE

LET'S HOPE THEY DO A BETTER JOB OF KEEPING THEM IN JAIL THIS TIME.

BWOOOOOOOOoo

OH, I DON'T KNOW.

POLICE

GOING AFTER THOSE TWO IS GREAT FOR STAYING IN SHAPE!

PSSSHHHH

GULK

TUNK
TUNK
TUNK

27 THWARTED CRIMES IN A SINGLE WEEK?

MUST BE SOME KIND OF A RECORD!

REMARKABLE MAN!

THE SAME. GLAD TO FINALLY MEET YOU, GUINEA PIG GIRL.

I TRUST YOU'VE HEARD OF MY COLLEAGUES...

...TALCUM POWDER LAD...

...AND MAHI-MAHI.

TO BE CONTINUED!

Well, Pam did an incredible job on the pages, which I think kind of proves five days is plenty of time for her part of the job. But I know better than to say that to her out loud.

We brought the issue in to Mrs. Maconie, and she's gonna deliver it to her friend at the Piffling Bugle, whose name is Lois something or other.

You two should be super proud of yourselves.

The artwork is outstanding. And, Eliot, I'm sure you would have had no way of knowing this...

...but there is nothing I'm happier to see on a menu than mahi-mahi.

Mrs. Maconie says if she hears anything from Lois, she'll let us know.

THE PIFFLING BUGLE

Proudly Serving the Communities of Piffling,
Blemish, and Goosefat Junction

Lois Watterson
Classified Ads
Obituaries
Funny Pages

Dear Eliot & Pam,

Bam! Pow! What can I say? This comic of yours really knocks me out! Can't wait for all the Bugle readers to see your work. It's been a while since we added something new to the funny pages, and I think your unique brand of screwball daffiness is just what the doctor ordered!

Eliot, I don't know where you get your ideas, but wherever it is, you better put an X on the map and keep going back there, because this stuff is gold!

Pam, your artwork is the bee's knees, and then some! It reminds me of one of our longest-running comic strips: Darn You Kids, by Gladys Smylie. And believe you me, that's high praise indeed!

I'm planning to run this first issue in Monday's edition, so make sure to tell your friends and family (so they can buy a stack of extra copies)!!

Toodles!
Lois

OK, this is it. By this time tomorrow, The Mighty Onion will be in the white-hot glare of the media spotlight, its plotline being dissected by people all across the greater Piffling region (to say nothing of Blemish and Goosefat Junction).

I wish Mrs. Maconie hadn't pointed out to me that the Piffling Bugle has a "Letters to the Editor" section. I mean, come on: criticism of my work, viewable by everyone in town? They might as well bring back public executions!

Well, well, well. What have we here?

A new comic in the Piffling Bugle?

Excellent. I've been LOOKING for something like this...

...TO TEAR TO PIECES IN MY BLOG!!!

SUNDAY

WELL, TOMORROW'S THE BIG DAY: THE MIGHTY ONION IS GONNA BE PRINTED UP AS A SPECIAL FEATURE IN THE PIFFLING BUGLE. MY NAME, IN PRINT! I CAN'T EVEN BELIEVE IT.

TODAY I WAS TELLING MELANIE HOW EXCITING ALL THIS WAS FOR ME, AND SUDDENLY SHE WAS LIKE:

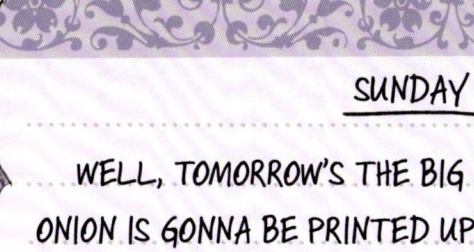

PAM, WHEN YOU'RE A WORLD-FAMOUS COMIC BOOK ARTIST...

PROMISE ME YOU WON'T FORGET ALL THE LOSERS YOU USED TO BE FRIENDS WITH.

SO I SAID:

LISTEN TO ME: I WILL ALWAYS BE THERE FOR YOU...

...MALORIE.

THEN WE BOTH LAUGHED SO HARD, THERE WAS SNOT COMING OUT OF OUR NOSES.

THE PIFFLING BUGLE

FUNNY PAGES

STARTING TODAY: THE MIGHTY ONION

We here at the *Bugle* proudly present our newest feature, a comic book story created by local middle schoolers Eliot Quigly and Pamela Jones. We know you're going to love it—BAM! POW!—just as much as we do. Enjoy!

MONDAY

THE WAITING IS OVER: TODAY, THE MIGHTY ONION WAS PRINTED IN THE PIFFLING BUGLE FOR THE FIRST TIME! ALL THE KIDS AT SCHOOL WERE TALKING ABOUT IT, AND EVEN ELIOT SEEMED HAPPY, FOR ONCE.

I MEAN, YEAH, THEY PRINTED IT IN BLACK AND WHITE, WHICH WAS KIND OF DISAPPOINTING. AND THERE ARE SO MANY ADS, IT SOMETIMES LOOKED LIKE GUINEA PIG GIRL WAS FIGHTING CRIME AT PEKING PALACE. BUT ALL IN ALL, IT'S A GREAT START.

ELIOT SAYS HE WON'T BE ABLE TO RELAX UNTIL HE SEES WHAT THE READERS HAVE TO SAY.

Letters to the Editor

To the editor,

This past Monday marked the launch of the *Bugle*'s new comic book feature, *The Mighty Onion*. I was skeptical at first, as I have had my doubts about the editorial direction of the Funny Pages ever since the paper saw fit to cancel my favorite comic strip, *Sassafras Sam*.

But I must say *The Mighty Onion* was not nearly as disappointing as I expected it to be. I'll be looking forward to seeing what happens next, especially if it involves bringing back Sassafras Sam.

Beatrice Gloiker
Blemish

Letters to the Editor

To the editor,

I just finished reading the first installment in the *Bugle*'s new comic book feature, *The Mighty Onion*, and wanted to share my thoughts.

Hats off to these two youngsters, Eliot Quigly and Pamela Jones, for seizing the initiative and launching their own newspaper feature.

It reminds me of the chutzpah my chums and I had back in our schoolboy days, when we started a bootshining service in the alleyway next to the Bellevue Hotel. Let me tell you, back then hard work really meant something, and we were well pleased to toil from dawn to dusk just to win the prize of a shiny nickel at the end of the day.

Walt J. Snaffleburger
East Piffling

To the edito

OK, the reviews are in, and the Piffling Bugle readers seem to agree: The Mighty Onion is...

...well, to be honest, it's a little hard to understand what these people are even TALKING about half the time.

But at least no one seemed to completely hate it. And the editor lady gave us the go-ahead to make a new issue, so I guess that means I'd better go stock up on candy bars.

TODAY MRS. MACONIE TOLD ME THAT THE FUNNY PAGES EDITOR, LOIS WATTERSON, WANTS TO INVITE ME TO THE OFFICES OF THE PIFFLING BUGLE. SHE'D LIKE ME TO MEET GLADYS SMYLIE, THE CREATOR OF THE DARN YOU KIDS COMIC STRIP, WHICH HAS BEEN RUNNING IN THE PAPER SINCE, LIKE, THE GREAT DEPRESSION OR SOMETHING.

JUST ME? WHAT ABOUT ELIOT?

HM. NOW THAT YOU MENTION IT, SHE DIDN'T SAY ANYTHING ABOUT ELIOT.

I'LL DOUBLE-CHECK ABOUT THAT.

SURE ENOUGH, IT TURNS OUT THE INVITE IS JUST FOR ME AND NO ONE ELSE. SO WHO KNOWS WHAT THAT'S ALL ABOUT? GUESS I'LL FIND OUT ON FRIDAY.

WHEN I TOLD MOM THAT I WAS GONNA MEET GLADYS SMYLIE, SHE GOT ALL EXCITED AND RAN UPSTAIRS TO THE ATTIC. WHEN SHE CAME BACK, SHE HAD THIS BOX OF OLD STUFF SHE KEPT FROM WHEN SHE WAS A LITTLE GIRL.

I LOVED DARN YOU KIDS WHEN I WAS YOUR AGE.

I USED TO CLIP OUT MY FAVORITES AND SAVE THEM.

SURE ENOUGH, SHE HAD A WHOLE STACK OF THESE OLD COMIC STRIPS. LIKE 30 OR 40 OF THEM.

BOY, OH BOY, DID THESE THINGS MAKE ME LAUGH!

HEE HEE!

Today when I got home from school, Mom handed me this old paperback she found at a yard sale the next block over.

Talk about luck! There's no WAY I would have found this...

...if they hadn't accidentally thrown it in with the romance novels.

To be honest, I was all set to do my usual thing: act grateful and then chuck it in the trash when Mom wasn't looking.

But then I started flipping through the thing and reading a few words here and there. And, hey, I gotta admit, this Jack Baccarat dude seems to know what he's talking about when it comes to comics.

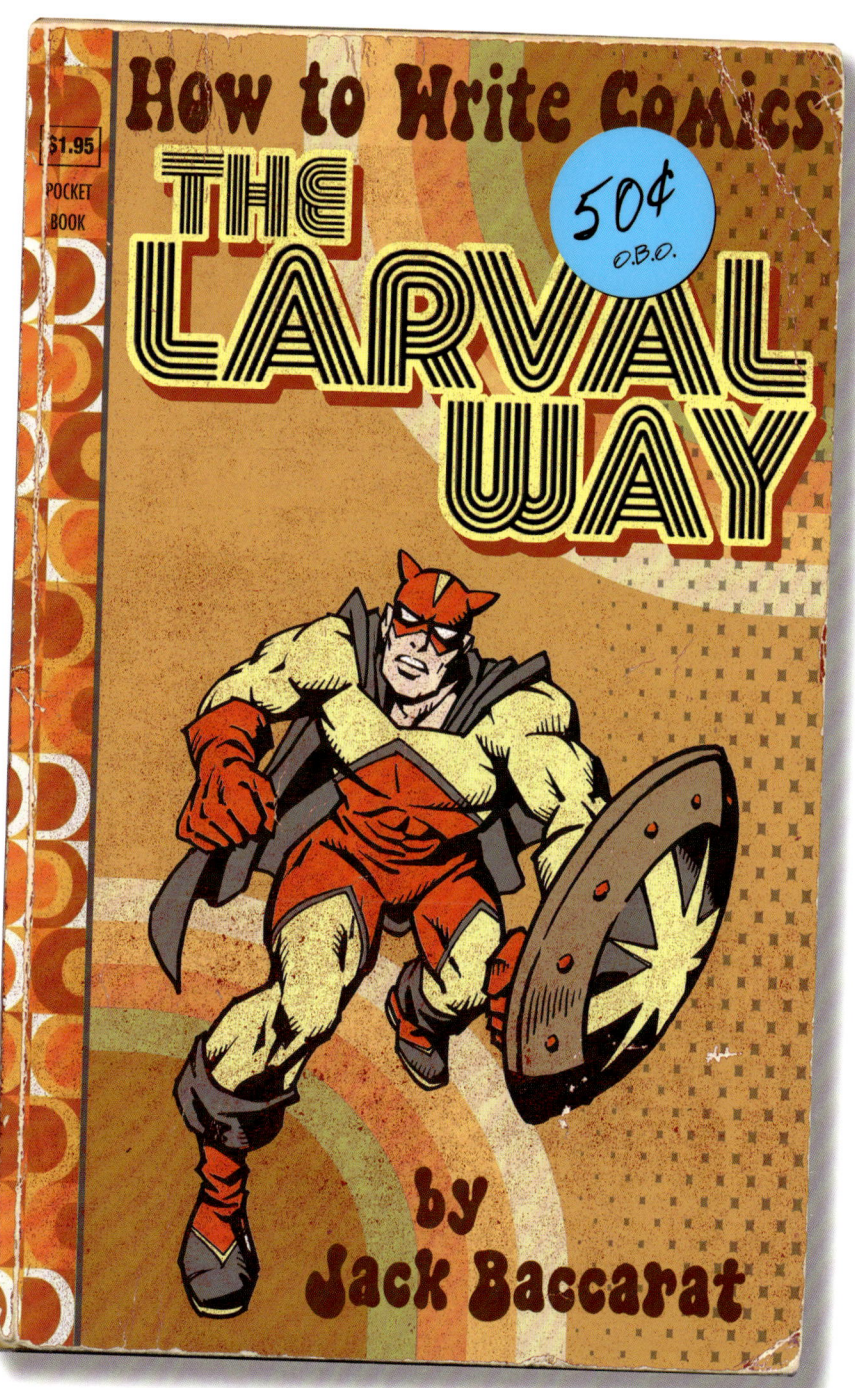

CHAPTER 3

Raising the Stakes

Now, let me tell you, kids.

I didn't get to be head honcho at Larval Comics by going with the flow. No, even back when I started out in 1948, it knew it was time for something new in the world of comics, and that something was this: STAKES.

No, I ain't talkin' about Ribeye. I mean giving the superheroes serious calamities to deal with. See, back then, writers were content to have the heroes keep clobbering small-time crooks all day. If it wasn't that, it was rescuing kittens, for cryin' out loud! Can you *imagine*?

Anyway, first day on the job, I called all the writers into my office, and I said, "Enough with burglars stealing diamonds, already. Gimme some spectacle, and I mean Godzilla-scale!" It was good advice back then, and trust me, it's even more on the money right now in 1975.

25

So, yeah. Old Jack Baccarat has got me rethinking my whole approach to this comics-writing game. It's time to go big or go home!

Today I tossed out my plan to have Sid and Rocky break out of jail again to steal an incredibly valuable tiara. What I need is for the Mighty Onion and Guinea Pig Girl to go up against, like, the most dangerous thing that a human being can even imagine.

German shepherds?

Anyway, I'm gonna sleep on it, and hopefully by tomorrow morning, it'll hit me.

Pam, good news: I got super inspired last night and was able to finish the next script.

NICE! DOES THIS MEAN I'M GONNA BE DRAWING MAHI-MAHI AGAIN?

For sure. But wait until you see what they're up against this time.

LADIES AND GENTLEMEN, I PROUDLY PRESENT TO YOU: THE CRAFTY KOALA!

LOL. You're never gonna let me live that down, are you? No, we're going BIG this time. Like, Godzilla-scale.

SERIOUSLY? THAT SOUNDS LIKE IT'S GONNA TAKE ME A LONG TIME TO DRAW.

Not gonna lie: It probably will. But come on. We're in the Piffling Bugle now. Time to raise the stakes!

ANYTHING ELSE I SHOULD KNOW ABOUT?

Let's put it this way: I hope you like drawing monsters that have eight legs. And, like, Los Angeles in ruins.

HATE YOU.
HATE YOU SO MUCH.

<u>FRIDAY</u>

WOW, WHAT A DAY! IN THE MORNING ELIOT GAVE ME HIS LATEST SCRIPT, AND I GOTTA SAY: HE REALLY IS TAKING THINGS TO THE NEXT LEVEL NOW.

BUT THE BIG NEWS IS WHAT HAPPENED AFTER SCHOOL WHEN MRS. MACONIE TOOK ME OVER TO MEET LOIS WATTERSON AND GLADYS SMYLIE. WE WERE SITTING IN THIS CONFERENCE ROOM, LOOKING AT SOME OF GLADYS'S ORIGINAL ART, AND THEN SUDDENLY THE TWO OF THEM WERE LIKE:

SO, PAM, GLADYS IS AT A STAGE IN HER LIFE WHERE SHE'S—

I WANT YOU TO TAKE OVER THE DRAWING DUTIES ON DARN YOU KIDS.

WHADDYA SAY?

I MEAN, MY JAW WAS ON THE FLOOR. THEY SAID THEY COULD SEE, LOOKING AT MY WORK, THAT I'D BE THE PERFECT NEW ARTIST FOR THE STRIP. AND SINCE DARN YOU KIDS IS, LIKE, SYNDICATED OR WHATEVER, THAT MEANS IT RUNS IN NEWSPAPERS ALL ACROSS THE COUNTRY.

I TOLD THEM I HAD A WHOLE ISSUE OF THE MIGHTY ONION TO GET DONE FIRST, AND GLADYS WAS LIKE, "TAKE ALL THE TIME YOU NEED."

I STAYED QUIET, BUT IN MY HEAD THE DECISION WAS ALREADY MADE. HOW COULD I PASS THIS UP?

DOES THIS SEEM LIKE A PLACE YOU COULD GET USED TO?

IT'S INCREDIBLE!

IF I WERE A MEMBER OF THE COMMITTEE, I'D WANT TO STAY HERE ALL THE TIME!

WELL, I'LL LET YOU IN ON A LITTLE SECRET:

I'VE SPONSORED YOUR CANDIDACY PERSONALLY...

...AND I'LL BE BRINGING IT UP FOR A VOTE AT THE END OF THE MONTH.

MOMENTS LATER, OUR HEROES HAVE JOINED KEY MEMBERS OF THE JUSTICE COMMITTEE...

...AS THEY RACE TO CALIFORNIA TO CONFRONT A DISASTER THAT HAS STRUCK LOS ANGELES.

IT'S GROK-TOPUS. HE'S ON A RAMPAGE IN THE HEART OF THE CITY.

HIS BODY CONTAINS EIGHT BRAINS...

ONE LOCATED IN THE TIP OF EACH TENTACLE.

WE'RE GONNA HAVE TO SPLIT UP.

TO BE CONTINUED!

There's no getting around it: Pam and I are finally hitting our stride. The latest issue went out in the paper this past week, and the response has been incredible. Even the Piffling Bugle readers are starting to get with the program. Like this one:

THE PIFFLING BUGL

Letters to the Editor

To the editor,
Just wanted to say how glad I am that the paper took a chance on this new comic book feature, *The Mighty Onion*. The latest installment really won me over with its manic pacing and its defiant refusal to adhere to any form of story logic.
My favorite moment was the "Onion Puffs" plot turn: a very clever critique of the modern American salty snack industry and its reliance on additives and artificial flavorings. Nicely done!

Lloyd Pewkerman
Piffling

To the editor,
In all my years of reading the *Bugle*, no article has angered me so much as "Asparagus: Studies

Sure, I didn't mean for the Onion Puffs to be a critique of anything. But, hey, Lloyd was into it, and that's good enough for me.

WELL, THERE'S NO TURNING BACK NOW. TODAY
I TOLD LOIS WATTERSON THAT I WOULD AGREE TO
BECOME THE NEW DARN YOU KIDS ARTIST. MAN,
I HAVE NEVER SEEN A MIDDLE-AGED LADY SO
HYPED UP ABOUT SOMETHING.

I ASKED LOIS IF SHE HAD EVER WRITTEN JOKES
BEFORE, AND SHE STARTED TALKING ABOUT ALL
THE FUNNY TV SHOWS SHE'S A FAN OF, AND HOW
SHE ONCE MADE EVERYONE LAUGH WHEN THEY
WERE PLAYING PINOCHLE.

Hey, Pam, wanna go for bubble tea after school? My treat! ☺

OH WOW, MELANIE. I WISH I COULD, BUT I'M SO BUSY RIGHT NOW. ☹

Mighty Onion pages? BTW loved the latest issue. So exciting!

THANKS! ACTUALLY IT'S SOMETHING ELSE, BUT THEY TOLD ME NOT TO TALK ABOUT IT YET.

OK, Mystery Girl. ☺ How about this weekend? I've got a coupon that's about to expire.

YEAH, I DON'T KNOW.
IS THERE SOMEONE ELSE
YOU COULD GO WITH?

No problem. Just let me
know when you've completed
this top secret mission
you're on, OK? ☺

THANKS FOR
UNDERSTANDING.
YOU'RE THE BEST!

Well, I am pretty
freaking amazing, can't
argue with that. ☺
See you around!

FOR SURE!
GROWL AT THE BUBBLE
TEA LADY FOR ME, OK?

LOL!

CHAPTER 9

Humanizing Your Heroes

Sure, we love seeing our favorite heroes in action, but it can't be all action, all the time. (Trust me, I tried it once, in an issue of *Cage Fighters Unlimited*. Nothing but the sound of crunching bones for seventy straight pages. Ha! The fans wanted to string me up. I ain't kiddin'.)

No, the readers of today want their heroes to be real flesh-and-blood mortals: human beings who they can relate to. So how do you achieve this as a writer? Well, here's a little trick that's served me well: **Give your hero a nickname.**

Back when I invented Toaster Oven Man, I'll level with you: The sales were headed straight into the toilet. But then, around issue 13, I had Potassium Girl call him "Toasty," and—BAM!— something just clicked. Two hundred issues later, I guess you could say I made the right decision.

67

So here's another huge game changer, courtesy of old Jack Baccarat: nicknames.

I mean, if that was what kept a stinker like Toaster Oven Man in print, then just think what it could do for a comic that's actually good, like The Mighty Onion.

So now all I need to do is think of a decent nickname for "Guinea Pig Girl."

I'll just say this: Giving the advice is a whole lot easier than following it.

TODAY LOIS WATTERSON HAD ME STOP BY THE OFFICES OF THE PIFFLING BUGLE AFTER SCHOOL. SHE GAVE ME A FOLDER FILLED WITH PICTURES BY GLADYS SMYLIE, SHOWING ME HOW TO DRAW THE ENTIRE CAST OF DARN YOU KIDS.

THERE ARE MAINLY JUST 12 CHARACTERS YOU NEED TO BE ABLE TO DRAW.

WIGGY, CHESTER, CORKY, MAUDE, GILBERT, SKUNKY, WILLARD, BESSIE, SNEEZER, DIMPLE, POOKIE, AND JOE.

LOIS NOTICED I WAS HYPERVENTILATING, SO SHE TOLD ME SHE'D FOCUS MOSTLY ON WIGGY, GILBERT, BESSIE, AND JOE. I PROMISED I'D GET GOOD AT DRAWING THOSE FOUR CHARACTERS WITHIN THE NEXT COUPLE WEEKS.

Hey, Pam. You ready to roll with the next issue? I just put the finishing touches on the latest script.

SURE. THESE PAGES MAY TAKE ME A LITTLE LONGER, JUST SO YOU KNOW.

Understood. Can't be easy drawing Grok-topus. Next time I'll invent a creature with fewer legs!

NO, I MEAN I'VE GOT OTHER STUFF I'M WORKING ON THAT'S GONNA SLOW THINGS DOWN A LITTLE.

Other stuff? What kind of other stuff are we talking about here?

THERE'S MORE GOING ON IN MY LIFE THAN THE COMIC, ELIOT, OK?

We worked hard to get here, Pam. If we fall behind schedule, Lois is not gonna be happy.

I'VE TALKED WITH LOIS. SHE'S COOL WITH IT.

Wait, you've been talking to Lois? Since when? And how come I'm only finding out about this NOW?

WILL YOU CALM DOWN? I'LL HAVE THE PAGES DONE AS SOON AS I CAN. EVERYTHING'S FINE.

OK, whatever. So what do you think of "Guinny" as a nickname for Guinea Pig Girl?

YOU'VE BEEN READING THAT JACK BACCARAT BOOK, HAVEN'T YOU?

MONDAY

WELL, I DON'T KNOW WHAT TO SAY ABOUT
MY SO-CALLED WEEKEND, OTHER THAN THAT IT
INVOLVED WAKING UP, DRAWING, DRAWING, DRAWING,
AND THEN, AFTER DRAWING A LITTLE MORE, GOING
TO BED (AROUND 2 AM).

"LET'S MAKE A
COMIC BOOK TOGETHER,"
HE SAID.

"IT'LL BE FUN,"
HE SAID.

MGRRRRR

BUT I MANAGED TO GET ALL THE MIGHTY
ONION PAGES DONE, AND SOMEHOW STILL HAD A
LITTLE TIME LEFT OVER FOR THE PRACTICE I
NEEDED DRAWING WIGGY AND BESSIE.

IT WAS ALL WORTH IT, THOUGH, WHEN I WENT
IN TO SHOW MY WORK TO LOIS WATTERSON.

I PROBABLY SHOULD HAVE TOLD ELIOT ABOUT THIS WHOLE DARN YOU KIDS THING BY NOW, BUT I KEEP CHICKENING OUT. HE'S NOT GONNA TAKE IT WELL. (I MEAN, HE NEVER TAKES ANYTHING WELL, BUT I'M AFRAID THIS ONE COULD REALLY SEND HIM OFF THE DEEP END.)

ANYWAY, THE NEW ISSUE OF THE MIGHTY ONION RUNS IN THE PAPER TOMORROW. HOPEFULLY THAT WILL KEEP HIM IN A GOOD MOOD.

THE MIGHTY ONION

ISSUE 3

Written by Eliot Quigly
Drawings by Pamela Jones

WHEN WE LAST SAW OUR HERO, HE'D BEEN KNOCKED TO THE GROUND BY THE DREADED GROK-TOPUS...

SHHAAAAAA

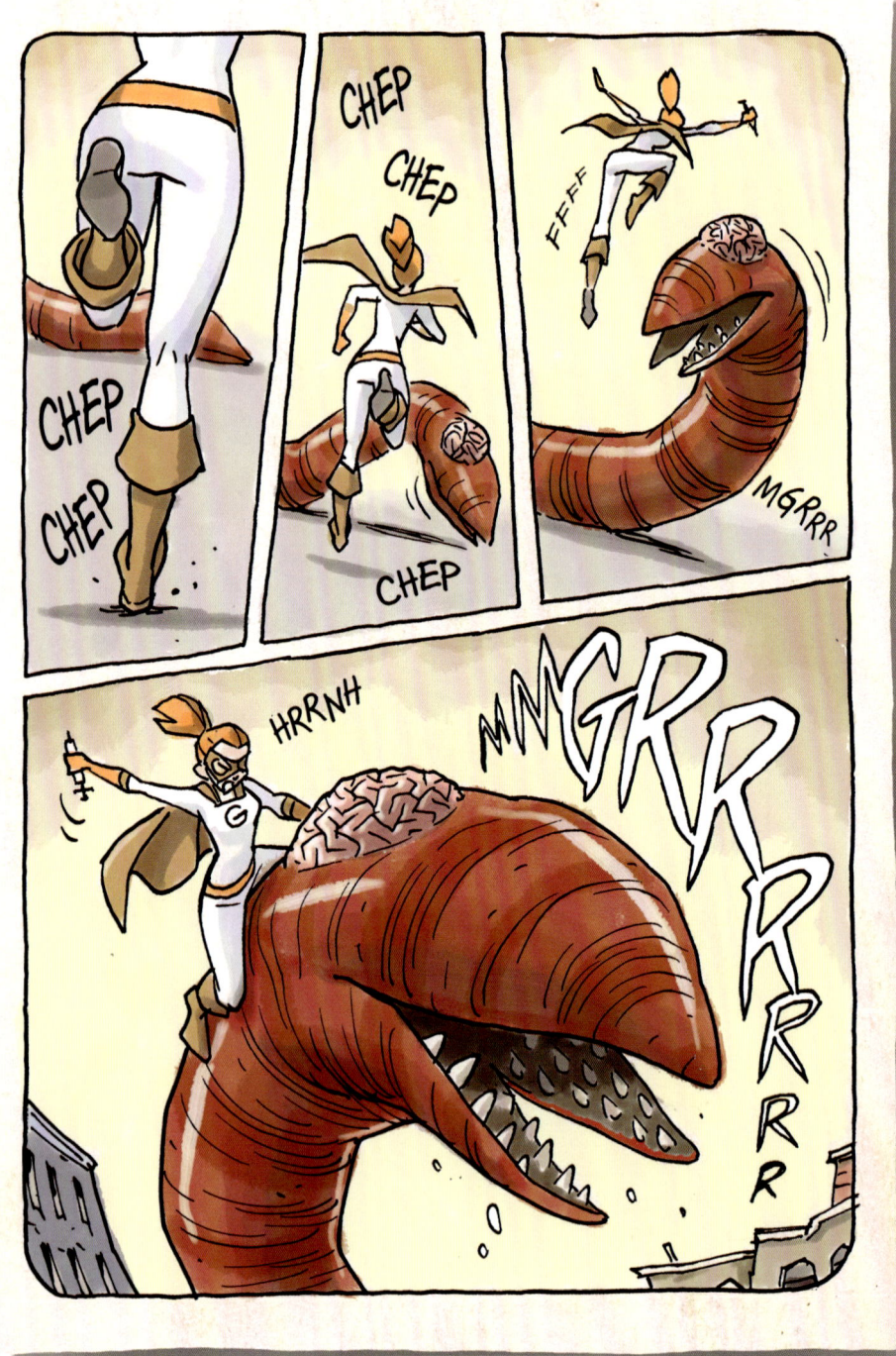

SURE ENOUGH, THE VERY NEXT DAY GUINEA PIG GIRL WINS HER COMMITTEE MEMBERSHIP BY WAY OF A UNANIMOUS VOTE.

...AND SO, BY VIRTUE OF THE POWERS VESTED IN ME...

...I HEREBY DECLARE GUINEA PIG GIRL TO BE A FULL-FLEDGED MEMBER OF THE JUSTICE COMMITTEE!

KLAP

KLAP

KLAP

KLAP

KLAP

KLAP

KLAP

KLAP

LATER, AFTER THE CEREMONY...

CONGRATULATIONS, GUINEA PIG GIRL. AND WELCOME TO THE TEAM.

THANK YOU, TALCUM POWDER LAD.

PLEASE. WE'RE FRIENDS NOW.

CALL ME TALC.

IT'S ALL BEEN SUCH A WHIRLWIND. I JUST...

CAN'T BELIEVE IT'S REALLY HAPPENING.

SAY, WHAT'RE YOU DOING THIS WEEKEND?

'CAUSE A FEW OF US ARE PLANNING A SKIING TRIP.

IN THE ALPS.

OH WOW.

THAT SOUNDS AMAZING.

YEAH.

YEAH, I'D DEFINITELY BE UP FOR THAT.

TO BE CONTINUED!

Well, I guess this is what they call living the dream. Because today at school Mrs. Maconie came up and handed me a postcard that had come into the offices of the Piffling Bugle. A postcard that was mailed...

...FROM OUT OF STATE!!!

Turns out some dude who lives in Whitless, Minnesota, gets copies of the paper mailed to him. I mean, come on: This is not an isolated incident. It can't be. The Mighty Onion is

SWEEPING THE NATION!!

GREETINGS from WHITLESS MINN.

USA / FORNEVER

Hemlock

POISONOUS PLANTS

WHITLESS ... APR 2 ... MINN.

Eliot Quigly & Pam Jones
c/o The Piffling Bugle
502 Main Street
Piffling, IN 47348

Dear Eliot & Pam,
Congratulations on The
Mighty Onion. I've been
reading the Piffling Bugle
funny pages for many, many
years now, and I must tell you
your comic is probably the
best thing they've ever run
(with the possible exception
of Sassafras Sam).
Keep up the great work!

Herb Marjoram

I showed the postcard to Pam and was telling her my theory about how many other readers we've probably got, coast to coast. Halfway through, no kidding: She YAWNED!

Mrs. Maconie says we're going to have a pizza party tomorrow, during which she'll be making a big announcement. I couldn't get her to spill the beans, but I'm pretty sure what's going on: It's gotta be that the Bugle wants to start running The Mighty Onion in full color. Just wait till everyone sees Pam's artwork the way it was intended. MINDS WILL BE BLOWN!!

WEDNESDAY

I SWEAR I WAS GONNA TELL HIM. I WAS ALL SET TO GO UP TO ELIOT AFTER SCHOOL TODAY AND EXPLAIN TO HIM ABOUT GLADYS SMYLIE AND WHY I'VE BEEN SO BUSY LATELY.

SO NATURALLY MRS. MACONIE HAD TO STAND UP IN THE MIDDLE OF THE PIZZA PARTY AND GO:

OK, HERE'S THE BIG NEWS I PROMISED YOU ALL...

...PAM IS GOING TO BE THE NEW ARTIST ON DARN YOU KIDS!

CAN YOU BELIEVE IT?

ELIOT LOOKED AT ME AS IF SHE'D JUST ANNOUNCED THAT I WAS A PUPPY MURDERER. I WANTED TO TALK TO HIM, BUT SUDDENLY, I WAS SURROUNDED BY ALL THESE KIDS CONGRATULATING ME. BY THE END OF CLASS, THOUGH, HE SEEMED TO HAVE CALMED DOWN. MAYBE HE'LL SURPRISE ME AND BE MORE MATURE ABOUT THINGS THAN HE USUALLY IS.

PAM IS A LYING, BACKSTABBING, POO-POO HEAD!!!

After all I've done for her, you'd think she'd have some sense of loyalty. BUT NO! The minute someone waltzes in with a shiny new opportunity, she's like:

I don't know what I can do, other than turn to the one guy in this world who seems to have all the answers.

CHAPTER 15

This Time, It's Personal

I remember years ago I called one of the writers into my office after I'd read his latest script. "Frank, I gotta hand it to you: This fight scene between Whip-poor-will and Mister Superbia is dynamite. How'd you come up with it?"

I'll never forget how red his face got. "Well, my brother-in-law and I got into this big shouting match last weekend about who's better between the Yankees and the Mets. I guess some of that stuff found its way into the script."

Sure, comic books are filled with laser beams and guys in latex. But the truth is, it's all about drawing from your own personal experience. No comic I've ever read was worth a hill of beans if it wasn't based on something the writer really went through.

So next time life throws you a curveball, just

113

As always, Jack Baccarat provides the trail of bread crumbs in this twisted maze we call creativity.

Pam landing the Darn You Kids gig may seem like a setback for our comic, but it doesn't have to be that way. Not if I can use it as INSPIRATION for my writing.

I gotta say, there's nothing quite so therapeutic as dumping all your frustrations and insecurities into a work of fiction.

Schmerple
LAWN CARE, INC.

1 800 NO WEEDZ

"Don't just fertilize it.
SCHMERPLE-ize it!"

Pam,

Just wanted to add a little note with this latest script to clarify a couple things. On pages 4 and 5, pay special attention to the emotions of the scene. The Mighty Onion has been badly mistreated, and we need to feel sympathy for him, big-time. Also we want the readers to be super disappointed by what a selfish, insensitive opportunist Guinea Pig Girl has turned out to be.

On the last page, when we get to the bad guy's mountain lair, I want you to really pull out the stops with the detail. This one page may take you DAYS to complete, but trust me: It'll be worth it!

Eliot

Justin's Mom: "Oh, those poor men, I hope they'll be OK."

ELIOT, WHAT ARE YOU TRYING TO PULL WITH THE DIALOGUE IN THIS SCRIPT? IT'S RIDICULOUS!

What are you talking about? That stuff's GENIUS. Readers will love it, trust me.

GUINEA PIG GIRL IS SUPPOSED TO BE A HERO. YOU'VE GOT HER TALKING LIKE SHE'S IN LOVE WITH HERSELF. AND WHY IS SHE BEING SUCH A JERK TO THE MIGHTY ONION?!

Pam, a person's character changes over time—and not always for the better. You, of all people, should understand that.

WHAT'S THIS ABOUT ME SPENDING DAYS ON JUST A SINGLE PAGE? YOU MUST BE DREAMING!

Our readers expect
the artwork to get
more and more amazing.
That's just
human nature.

LISTEN, I'VE GOT DARN
YOU KIDS DEADLINES NOW.
I COULDN'T SIT AROUND ALL
DAY WORKING ON YOUR COMIC
EVEN IF I WANTED TO.

"My comic?" I thought
this was OUR comic,
Pam. OUR COMIC!

YOURS, OURS, WHATEVER.
WHY DOES EVERYTHING HAVE
TO BE A DRAMA-FEST WITH YOU
ALL THE TIME?

Look, I was exaggerating
when I said "days," OK? Just make
the mountain lair look cool.
That's all I'm saying.

I SHOULD HAVE KNOWN SOMETHING LIKE THIS WAS GONNA HAPPEN. LOIS SAID SHE NEEDED ALL OF THE FIRST TWENTY DARN YOU KIDS COMICS DONE BY FRIDAY. WHICH IS OF COURSE THE SAME DAY THE LATEST ISSUE OF THE MIGHTY ONION IS DUE!

NO GETTING AROUND IT: BY THE TIME I FINISHED ALL THE COMIC STRIPS FOR LOIS, I BARELY HAD ANY ENERGY LEFT FOR ALL THOSE MIGHTY ONION PAGES. LUCKILY, I CAME UP WITH A GREAT WAY OF GETTING THE FINAL TWO PAGES FINISHED SUPER QUICKLY. THE LAST ONE ONLY TOOK ME LIKE FIVE MINUTES!

Usually Pam shows me the finished pages before she hands them in to Lois at the Piffling Bugle, but everything was so last minute this time, she said she just couldn't do that.

So I had to settle for her describing the pages to me at school.

So, yeah. Guess I won't see how this issue turned out until everyone else does: on the day it's printed in the actual newspaper.

THE MIGHTY ONION

ISSUE 4

Written by Eliot Quigly
Drawings by Pamela Jones

THE MIGHTY ONION, FINALLY GETTING A BREAK FROM HIS HEROIC DUTIES, IS ENJOYING A QUIET DAY AT HOME AS MILD-MANNERED TEENAGER, JUSTIN SQUIBBLY.

NRRFF

GUINEA PIG GIRL!

WE MEET AGAIN...

THERE HE IS ABLE TO ADMINISTER FIRST AID TO GUINEA PIG GIRL.

THANKS, MY FRIEND.

THAT WAS A CLOSE ONE.

BUT THERE'S NO TIME TO LOSE.

WE'VE GOT TO GET TO CAPTAIN MIGRAINE'S MOUNTAIN LAIR AND RESCUE THOSE WORKERS!

BUT JUST AFTER LIFTOFF, A THICK MOUNTAIN FOG MOVES INTO THE AREA.

WUP WUP WUP WUP

WOW, I CAN BARELY SEE A THING!

ME EITHER.

LUCKILY, THE GUINEA COPTER COMES EQUIPPED WITH A MOUNTAIN-AVOIDING RADAR SYSTEM.

THANK GOODNESS. SEEMS LIKE THE FOG IS GETTING EVEN WORSE.

RIGHT?

THICK AS PEA SOUP!

MOMENTS LATER, THEY LAND SAFELY OUTSIDE CAPTAIN MIGRAINE'S MOUNTAIN LAIR.
LET'S GO AROUND TO THE WEST ENTRANCE.
IT'S NOT SO HEAVILY GUARDED.
GOOD IDEA, GUINNY.
WILL GUINEA PIG GIRL AND THE MIGHTY ONION SUCCEED IN THEIR DANGEROUS MISSION? TUNE IN NEXT TIME TO FIND OUT!
TO BE CONTINUED!

Letters to the Editor

To the editor,
I just had to write in about the complete mess that your *Mighty Onion* comic has become. Why were so many pages devoted to the heroes getting snippy with each other? I turn to the Funny Pages to be entertained, not to see two characters bickering.

Esme Luffins-Kwaller
West Blemish

Letters to the Editor

To the editor,
Look, I hate to rain on the parade of a couple middle schoolers, but maybe it's time to put an end to the adventures of Onion Boy and Hamster Girl (sic), and bring back a comic strip made by someone who knows what they're doing.

P.S. Like *Sassafras Sam*!

Giuseppe Ventilatte
Piffling

To the edito

TO: PAM

Everything Happens For a Reason

So let's hear the REASON why you RUINED MY STORY!!

A THICK MOUNTAIN
FOG?!
SERIOUSLY??!!

WHAT IN THE HECK ARE YOU TRYING
TO PULL HERE?! You've turned me into
the laughingstock of Piffling!

Now everyone in town thinks I came up with
this ludicrous "low visibility" idea. What am I
supposed to do? Get a megaphone and go
through the streets? "Hey, everybody! It wasn't
me! It was my LAZY ARTIST, who just didn't FEEL
like drawing the LAST TWO PAGES!!"

YOU OWE ME AN APOLOGY, PAM.
A TEARFUL ONE!
Eliot

<u>TUESDAY</u>

SO EXCITED! LOIS WATTERSON SAYS SHE'S
ARRANGED A RADIO INTERVIEW FOR ME TO HYPE
UP THE DEBUT OF OUR WORK ON DARN YOU KIDS!
THIS SATURDAY, SHE'S TAKING ME INTO THE STUDIOS
OF WPBJ SMOOTH JAZZ 103.7, WHERE I'LL BE
THE FEATURED GUEST OF TORI GREESE, HOST OF
"AIRING IT OUT."

WHEN I TOLD MOM, SHE WAS BASICALLY
DANCING AROUND THE ROOM.

HONEY, THIS
IS INCREDIBLE!

I MEAN, TORI
GREESE INTERVIEWS
SUPER-FAMOUS
PEOPLE.

LIKE, LIKE...

WHAT'S
THE NAME OF
THAT GUY? FROM
THAT SHOW?

MOM, I
HAVE NO
IDEA WHAT
YOU'RE
TALKING
ABOUT.

YOU KNOW! WITH
THE SUNGLASSES!

I'm starting to regret writing that angry letter to Pam. Let's be clear: I am 100% in the right, and she's 100% in the wrong. But she didn't write back, and, I don't know, things have been a little weird between us ever since I did that.

Anyway, the good news is, I'm feeling super optimistic about the future. This whole thing with Pam comes down to time management. Naturally, she'll get better and better at juggling these two projects in the months ahead, and everything will be great. Right?

You're invited

to ___Melanie___'s ~incredibly fun~ Birthday Party!

Hey, Pam, I know you're pretty busy these days, you famous comic strip superstar, you. :)

But I can't have a party without YOU there, come on! Really hope you can make it.

♡ M.

DATE: Saturday, April 13th

TIME: 2pm

84623 Linn...

(55) 2...

· Cookies will be baked!

Cookies will be eaten!

LET'S PARTY! it's my BIRTHDAY

HI MELANIE,

WOW, I AM SOOO SORRY I CAN'T MAKE IT TO
YOUR BIRTHDAY ON SATURDAY. THERE'S THIS
BIG RADIO INTERVIEW I'VE GOTTA DO THAT
AFTERNOON, AND THEN I GUESS THEY'RE
DOING SOME SORT OF PHOTO SHOOT.

I REALLY WANTED TO GIVE YOU A SPECIAL
PRESENT FOR YOUR BIRTHDAY, BUT WITH ALL
MY DEADLINES, IT JUST TOTALLY SLIPPED MY
MIND. SO HERE'S A GIFT CARD THAT I HOPE YOU
CAN USE TO GET YOURSELF SOMETHING NICE.

GAIN FOR I   TO YOUR
                   THERE!!

                   UR FRIEND
                   REVER,

                   PAM

Choose the Value
$5 - $30

Waldorf™

Buy stuff.

Then buy
more stuff.

Waldorf™

This card has no value until activated at register

WOW, TODAY WAS ONE OF THE MOST EXCITING DAYS OF MY ENTIRE LIFE. LOIS TOOK ME IN FOR THE "AIRING IT OUT" INTERVIEW, AND EVEN THOUGH I WAS SUPER NERVOUS, TORI GREESE WAS A TOTAL PRO AT GETTING ME TO RELAX.

YOU'LL BE GREAT, I CAN TELL.

TRUST ME: I SAY THE WRONG THING EVERY TWO OR THREE MINUTES.

THEN THE EDITORS GET RID OF IT, AND I COME OUT SMELLING LIKE A ROSE.

WHEN THE INTERVIEW WAS DONE, THEY TOOK ME OVER TO THE OFFICES OF THE PIFFLING BUGLE TO DO A PHOTO SHOOT WITH A REAL PROFESSIONAL PHOTOGRAPHER!

THE GUY'S NAME WAS ALFONSO. HE HAD A FUNNY WAY OF PRONOUNCING MY NAME.

AFTER WE WERE DONE, LOIS ASKED ME IF I WOULD AGREE TO DO A RIBBON-CUTTING CEREMONY TOMORROW OVER AT KING PINS, PIFFLING'S NEW GLOW-IN-THE-DARK BOWLING ALLEY.

I'VE NEVER HAD SUCH A FULL CALENDAR IN MY WHOLE LIFE. IT'S LIKE PEOPLE THINK I'M A LOCAL CELEBRITY NOW OR SOMETHING!

FUNNY PAGES!

STARTING TODAY: DARN YOU KIDS!

NEW

We here at the *Bugle* could not be more delighted to present the return of our longest running comic strip, Gladys Smylie's *Darn You Kids!* Thanks to the talents of Piffling natives Lois Watterson and Pam Jones, you will see Gilbert, Wiggy, Skunky, and the rest of the gang in brand-new strips running every day of the week starting today.

In other news, we will no longer be serializing *The Mighty Onion*. Bam! Pow! It sure was a lot of fun, though, wasn't it?

Darn You Kids! By LOIS WATTERSON & PAM JONES

WHY ARE FISH
NEVER PROUD OF

I DUNNO.
WHY?

BECAUSE THEY'RE
ALWAYS BELOW

SUNDAY

THE RIBBON-CUTTING THING WENT REALLY WELL. (APART FROM MY BOWLING. I PROBABLY SET A NEW WORLD RECORD FOR CONSECUTIVE GUTTER BALLS!)

AFTERWARD LOIS TOOK ME TO THE BUBBLE TEA PLACE, AND, WOW, THE LADY WHO RUNS THE SHOP WAS LIKE A COMPLETELY DIFFERENT PERSON. SHE WAS BASICALLY BRAGGING TO PEOPLE ABOUT HOW I WAS ONE OF HER REGULAR CUSTOMERS!

THEN I WENT OVER TO ELIOT'S HOUSE TO SEE
HOW HE WAS HANDLING THE BAD NEWS ABOUT HIS
COMIC GETTING CANCELED. HIS DAD TOLD ME
ELIOT WAS FEELING A LITTLE UNDER THE WEATHER,
AND BASICALLY HADN'T LEFT HIS ROOM FOR THE
WHOLE WEEKEND.

WHAT A WEIRD SITUATION. I'M SURE ELIOT THINKS
I'M TO BLAME FOR ALL OF THIS, EVEN THOUGH IT'S
NOT MY FAULT. I DO KIND OF FEEL BAD ABOUT HOW
THINGS TURNED OUT. (BUT SECRETLY I'M RELIEVED:
NOT HAVING TO DO MIGHTY ONION PAGES IS GOING TO
MAKE MY LIFE A WHOLE LOT EASIER!)

From the Desk of
Mrs. Maconie
Room 310, Gurgling Meadows Middle School

Dear Eliot & Pam,

I just wanted to tell you both how disappointed I was to hear that The Mighty Onion will no longer be running in the newspaper. I'm sure you both are quite upset about that, and I wish there were something I could do other than giving you moral support.

I am incredibly proud of you two— I really am. Remember that every red light eventually turns green. (And then turns red again, but try not to think about that.)

So here's my idea: What if we go back to doing things the way we did before? I'm sure all the kids here at Gurgling Meadows

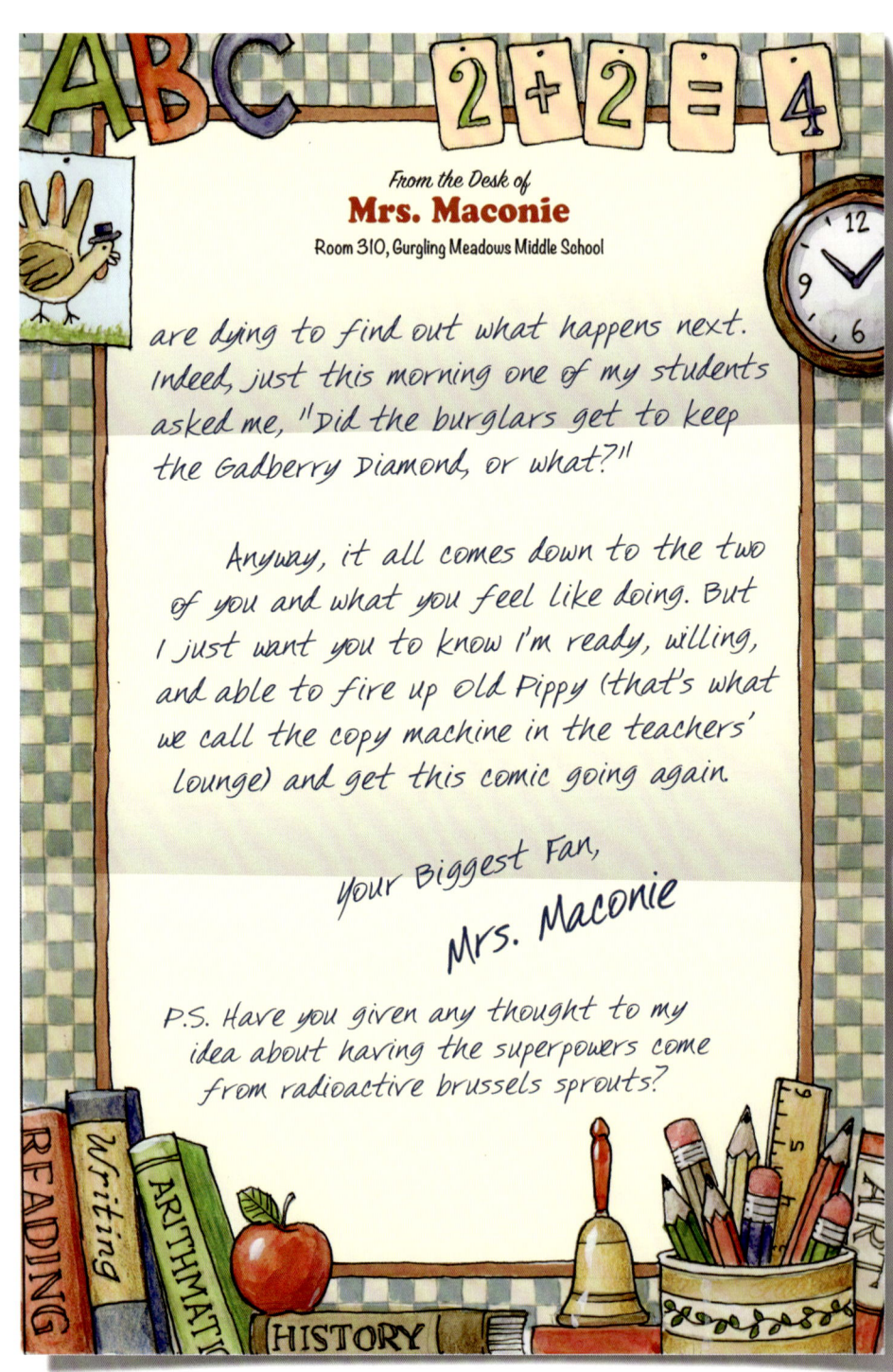

From the Desk of
Mrs. Maconie
Room 310, Gurgling Meadows Middle School

are dying to find out what happens next. Indeed, just this morning one of my students asked me, "Did the burglars get to keep the Gadberry Diamond, or what?"

Anyway, it all comes down to the two of you and what you feel like doing. But I just want you to know I'm ready, willing, and able to fire up old Pippy (that's what we call the copy machine in the teachers' lounge) and get this comic going again.

Your Biggest Fan,

Mrs. Maconie

P.S. Have you given any thought to my idea about having the superpowers come from radioactive brussels sprouts?

Life is funny. One day, it gives you big, golden opportunities, and then the next day, it comes along and tells you to smile so that it can haul off and kick out all your teeth. Life has a personal beef with me, is what I'm trying to say.

But maybe I'm made of sturdier stuff than I thought. Because this morning I woke up and I was like:

I mean, she didn't use those exact words, but I'm sure that's what she meant.

Pam, just wanted to touch base and see when you'll be ready to get started on the next issue.

ELIOT, I KNOW YOU WANT TO KEEP THE DREAM ALIVE. BUT I JUST DON'T HAVE THE KIND OF TIME I USED TO.

The Bugle was fun, sure. But I think we both got a little corrupted by "the Man," you know what I mean?

SO YOU WANT ME TO GO BACK TO SPENDING HOURS AND HOURS ON A COMIC THAT CAN ONLY BE READ BY KIDS AT SCHOOL?

Don't think of it that way. Think of it as getting back to our roots, Pam. Now's our chance to get lean and PUNK again.

I'D HELP YOU IF I COULD,
ELIOT. BUT LOIS NEEDS A
CONSISTENT LEVEL OF ENGAGE-
MENT FROM ME ON A DAILY BASIS.

Wow. So this is how it's
gonna be? I help you make
the leap to the big time,
then it's "So long, Eliot!"

OH, COME ON.
YOU'RE JUST TRYING TO GUILT
ME INTO DOING WHAT YOU WANT.
I'M TOO BUSY NOW, OK?
DEAL WITH IT.

Mark my words, Pam.
You're gonna regret this.
Don't come crawling back
to me when Darn You Kids
gets the axe!!

YOU DON'T KNOW ME
VERY WELL, DO YOU?
I DON'T CRAWL!

Forget what I said about Mrs. Maconie. She has never been right about anything. In MY world, the traffic lights go from green to red, and then they STAY red, and they just keep getting redder and redder until they explode into MASSIVE, GIGANTIC SUPERNOVAS OF REDNESS!!

GAAAH!

MY EYES!!

History will record this as the day I put down my writing pencil and never again picked it up: Tuesday, April something.

Dear Eliot!

Hi there! My name is Kitty Thorkelson! I'm a new student at Gurgling Meadows! You may have seen me in the halls by now. I'm the girl who's always wearing a magenta beret. Also, turquoise clogs. Can't go ANYWHERE without my trusty turquoise clogs! :)

Anyways, I happened to tell Mr. Budzinski what a comic book nerd I am, and he lent me his entire run of The Mighty Onion. Roughly 50 readings of all those issues later, I have to tell you it has completely changed my life! I mean, your writing is so incredible, I've had to invent a new word for it: Increbba-DOOBital! :)

But then, when I asked Mr. Budzinski if he had any more issues, he told me he wasn't sure if you were still doing them. Then he explained all about how the Piffling Bugle made this bizarre decision to stop running the series, and how your current artist has become busy with other stuff. (Which is a real head-scratcher to me, not gonna lie. How could ANYTHING be more important than The Onion of Mightiness?!?) :)

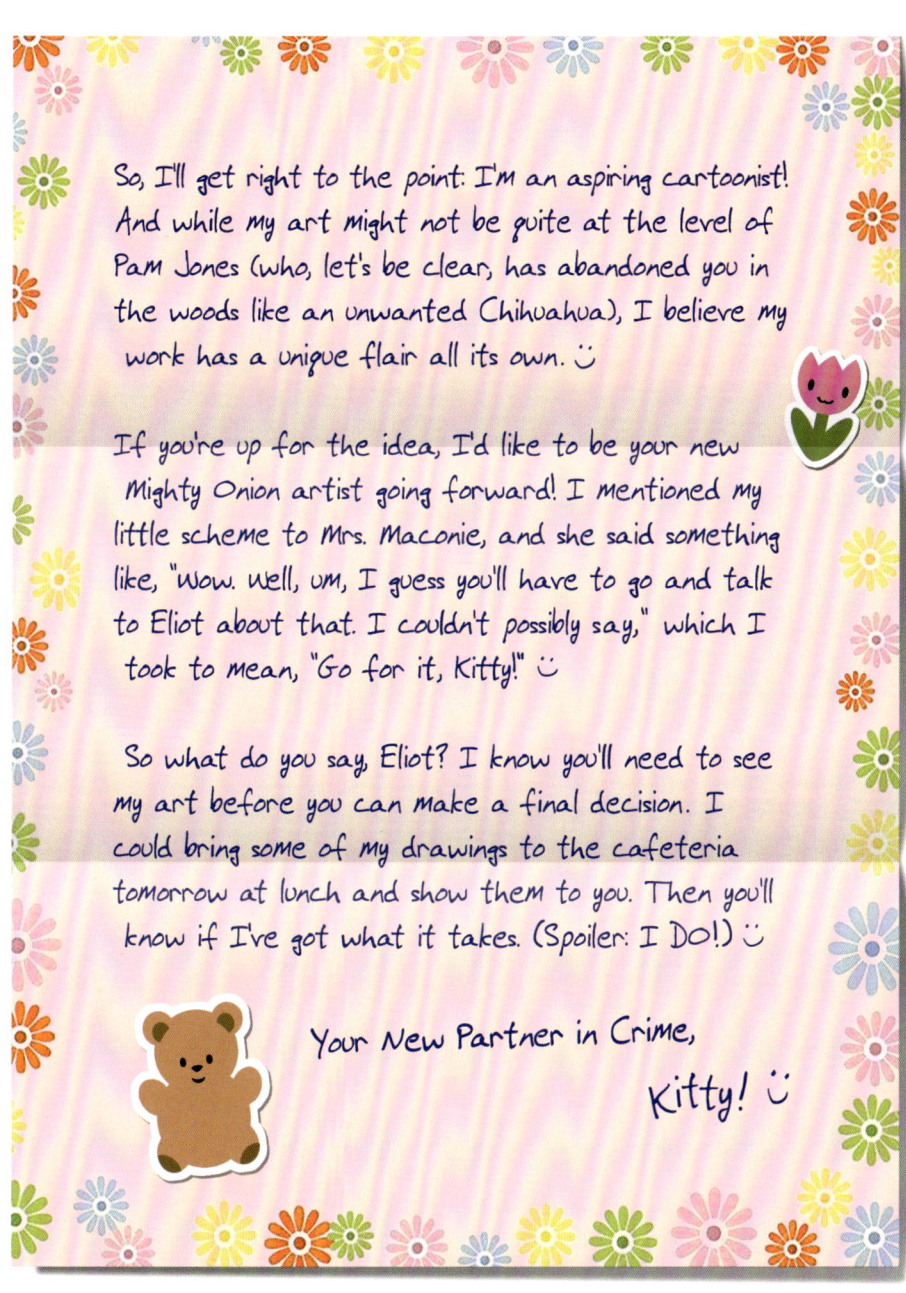

So, I'll get right to the point: I'm an aspiring cartoonist! And while my art might not be quite at the level of Pam Jones (who, let's be clear, has abandoned you in the woods like an unwanted Chihuahua), I believe my work has a unique flair all its own. ☺

If you're up for the idea, I'd like to be your new Mighty Onion artist going forward! I mentioned my little scheme to Mrs. Maconie, and she said something like, "Wow. Well, um, I guess you'll have to go and talk to Eliot about that. I couldn't possibly say," which I took to mean, "Go for it, Kitty!" ☺

So what do you say, Eliot? I know you'll need to see my art before you can make a final decision. I could bring some of my drawings to the cafeteria tomorrow at lunch and show them to you. Then you'll know if I've got what it takes. (Spoiler: I DO!) ☺

Your New Partner in Crime,

Kitty! ☺

133

Looks like I picked the wrong day to put down my writing pencil! Yesterday at school I got a look at the artwork of this transfer student named Kitty, who wants to be the new Mighty Onion artist. Now, I can't lie: Her style is super different from Pam's, and not in a good way. But here's the thing: She's a million times more enthusiastic about drawing comics than Pam ever was.

Actually, I have a number of issues with Kitty, right from the get-go.

But, hey, even a broken clock is right twice a day, and let's be honest: I am a clockless man at the moment.

So last night I sat down and hammered out a script for issue 5 of The Mighty Onion. Then this morning I brought it into school and handed it off to Kitty. Unlike Pam, she sat down and read the thing right away. And VERY unlike Pam, she had nothing but nice things to say about it.

Kitty says she works pretty quickly. So who knows, maybe she'll have all the pages done by the end of the week!

So Kitty handed over her pages today, and wow. It's like everything got sucked into a gigantic vortex of pink. She made all my characters look like preschoolers. Even Captain Migraine! What kind of person reads a script with a death scene in it and says, "I know: Let's make everything adorable!"

So, instead of drawing flowers, you just used...

...STICKERS of flowers.

Great, right?

Flower stickers are what I call "a signature flourish."

That's how you know it's an original Thorkelson.

Part of me wanted to just run home and bury all these pages at the bottom of my dresser drawer beneath the pants I've outgrown.

But I decided to show them to Mrs. Maconie and get a second opinion.

I think Kitty's artwork is charming.

I follow where the muse leads me, Mrs. Maconie. You know that.

What concerns me is your decision to have a beloved character plunge senselessly to her death.

Can we go back to talking about the stickers?

Anyway, she told me she's going to print it up and hand it out to all the students, but she wants me to consider taking a long break now. She said anyone reading between the lines could see I was in a weird place, emotionally.

I wanted to shout, "MY WHOLE **LIFE** IS A WEIRD PLACE, EMOTIONALLY!!" But I didn't. Grown-ups freak out when you yell stuff at them.

Dear Eliot and Kitty,

Well, congratulations, Eliot. You've discovered one of the most tried-and-true gimmicks in the comic book writer's classic bag of tricks: killing off a character. Very shrewd. This is guaranteed to get readers arguing and taking sides, and should win you a nice big bump in sales. (Yes, I realize no one actually pays money for your comic, but you get what I mean.)

The thing is, you're supposed to milk it for all it's worth over the course of at least four or five issues. Chucking her off a cliff in just one panel? I mean, I hate to say you blew it, but, Eliot: You blew it.

Your pal,
Leonard

Dear Eliot,

You may remember me as one of the first people to ever write you a fan letter. You even wrote me back. It was a very odd letter. But hey, you did write to me, so that was cool, I guess.

So here's the thing: Kitty's artwork is super cute. But what on earth is going on with the STORY? If it was between reading another issue like the one you just did and eating a huge bowl of French onion soup, not gonna lie: I would be reaching for the nearest spoon and a box of saltines.

Courtney

Stephanie Wellington

Dearest Elliot and "Kitty",

I decided to take a break from the novel I've been reading (The Depth of My Shallowness, by H. R. Stophinpuff) so as to take in your latest Mighty Onion comic. As I'm sure you're aware, it marks a startling departure from your earlier efforts, in both its aesthetics and its themes.

Gone is the whimsy and divertingly droll humor. In its place we find chaotic acts of violence and a protagonist who abandons honor in favor of wallowing in self-pity. In short, it would remind me of the critically-acclaimed novels I normally read, were it not so poorly conceived and executed in every respect.

I implore you: Either return to your earlier approach, or take pity on your readers by ceasing publication altogether.

With a heavy heart,

Stephanie

So the verdict is in, and, as usual, it's this: "Nicely done, Eliot—you've taken the cruddiest comic series in human history and somehow managed to make it even worse." When Kitty asked me to show her the fan mail, I had no choice but to lie.

Why does one lie always lead to another? I told her I was halfway done, but the truth is, I haven't written a single word. I feel like I've pulled up to the reddest red light of them all.

WEDNESDAY

WHAT IS IT WITH WRITERS? LOIS WATTERSON IS TURNING OUT TO BE JUST AS UPTIGHT ABOUT THINGS AS ELIOT WAS. YESTERDAY SHE MADE ME REDRAW ONE OF HER "HILARIOUS" GAGS BECAUSE I HAD WIGGY AND SNEEZER USING CELL PHONES INSTEAD OF OLD DIAL-UP THINGS WITH CORDS ON THEM.

I THOUGHT I'D MADE THIS CLEAR TO YOU, PAM.

DARN YOU KIDS IS ALL ABOUT NOSTALGIA.

IF IT DIDN'T EXIST IN THE 1950s, IT HAS NO PLACE IN THIS STRIP.

OH, AND SNEEZER WEARS DUNGAREES.

ALWAYS.

PERSONALLY, I THINK SHE SHOULD STOP WORRYING ABOUT THE DUNGAREES AND TRY HER HAND AT WRITING SOMETHING FUNNY. BUT I GUESS THAT'S ANOTHER THING THAT HAS NO PLACE IN THIS STRIP.

I thought we were

BEST FRIENDS

but now you're too
busy to spend any
time with me at all.

Oh well, I guess
nothing lasts

FOREVER

TO: MELANIE
FROM: PAM
Albatross
SORRY:
NO FANCY FOLDED TRICK MESSAGE IN HERE.
I DON'T PLAY GAMES LIKE THAT.

MELANIE,

WOW, WHERE DO I EVEN BEGIN?

FIRST OF ALL, WE ARE STILL BEST FRIENDS.
WE WILL ALWAYS BE BEST FRIENDS. JUST
BECAUSE I'M BUSY WITH ALL THIS COMIC
STRIP STUFF DOESN'T CHANGE THAT.

I'LL TELL YOU WHAT, THOUGH: YOU AND I
MAYBE HAVE A DIFFERENT IDEA OF WHAT
A FRIEND IS. BECAUSE IN MY WORLD, A FRIEND
IS UNDERSTANDING AND SUPPORTIVE AND
EAGER TO HELP YOU CHASE YOUR DREAMS.

I'M BUSY, OK? I MEAN, ALMOST TO THE POINT
OF BEING COMPLETELY OVERWHELMED. AND
YES, I CAN'T PUT AS MUCH TIME INTO OUR
FRIENDSHIP AS I USED TO. I'M SORRY ABOUT
THAT. I REALLY AM.

BUT AN ANGRY LETTER FROM YOU IS NOT
WHAT I NEED RIGHT NOW.

PAM

Yesterday, after another evening of watching TV instead of getting anything done on the next script, I sat in bed, reading old Jack Baccarat's book. I guess I was hoping for some inspiration that would get me writing again.

But boy did I get something different! I read this one part that was so totally on the money for my current situation, it was as if Jack himself was speaking directly to me.

You payin' attention, Eliot?!

'Cause I wrote this part for YOU.

YOOOU!!!

Calling It Quits

My old man always used to say to me, "Nothing lasts forever, Jack, except for dinner at Auntie Ethel's place every Thanksgiving."

Sure, anyone who's put in the hours cooking up a good comic book series wants it to keep going and going for as many years as possible.

But there's something to be said for bowing out at the top. If I've got one regret, it's that I waited too long to pull the plug on *The Nimrod Squad*. At its peak, it was a darn good read. But by the time I finally put it out of its misery, it wasn't good enough to even blow your nose into.

Sometimes your most sacred duty as a writer is knowing when to call it quits. If you feel like it's time to throw in the towel, that's probably because it is. Nobody likes it when people overstay their welcome. Not even Auntie Ethel.

191

Calling It Quits

My old man always used to say to me, "Nothing lasts forever, Jack, except f⸍⸍⸍⸍ tie Ethel's place ⸍⸍⸍

Su⸍⸍⸍ cooking up a g⸍⸍⸍ keep going ⸍⸍⸍ ssible.

But ⸍⸍⸍ ving out at the t⸍⸍⸍ vaited too long ⸍⸍⸍ quad. At its pe⸍⸍⸍ the time I fi⸍⸍⸍ 't good eno⸍⸍⸍

Somet⸍⸍⸍ riter is knowin⸍⸍⸍ quits. If you feel like it's time to throw in the towel, that's probably because it is. Nobody likes it when people overstay their welcome. Not even Auntie Ethel.

191

Don't fill up on snacks. We're going to Peking Palace tonight.

Last night, we all went out to Peking Palace for dinner. I guess my parents must have noticed that I was feeling down about things, and they thought a little General Tso's might cheer me up. You know what? A+ for effort. It shows they're at least paying attention.

As soon as we walked into the place, I could hear some kind of loud party going on in the back. Turns out it was a glitzy birthday bash for Gladys Smylie. And there's Pam right in the middle, laughing it up with all her new pals from the Piffling Bugle.

It is better to go out in a blaze of glory than to slowly fade away.

So there I was: stuck with my parents at Peking Palace, overhearing Pam in the next room having the time of her life, and reading a fortune that could have been ghostwritten by Jack Baccarat.

I mean, come on. This cookie was giving me a very stark choice. Was I gonna let The Mighty Onion slowly wither away into a flowery pink death spiral?

Or did I have the guts to put it out of its misery?

FRIDAY

LAST NIGHT I HAD TO GO TO THIS BIG BIRTHDAY THING FOR GLADYS SMYLIE AT PEKING PALACE. UGH! THREE HOURS OF THE WORLD'S MOST BORING PEOPLE STANDING UP AND MAKING LONG, POINTLESS SPEECHES. JUST WHEN I THOUGHT IT WAS FINALLY OVER AND WE COULD ALL GO HOME, THEY HAD GLADYS STAND UP FOR A BIG ROUND OF APPLAUSE. AND THEN **SHE** GOES INTO A SPEECH!

YOU KNOW, SEEING ALL OF YOU HERE TONIGHT REMINDS ME OF A REALLY FUNNY STORY.

BUT IN ORDER TO TELL THAT STORY, I HAVE TO TELL YOU A COUPLE OF **OTHER** STORIES FIRST···

SNRRR

SNRRR

I DON'T KNOW. THIS WHOLE PIFFLING BUGLE THING USED TO BE FUN. BUT NOW IT'S KIND OF TAKING OVER MY WHOLE LIFE. I HARDLY GET TO SEE MY FRIENDS ANYMORE. IT'S LIKE I DON'T EVEN **HAVE** FRIENDS NOW.

Hey, Pam. I just wanted to thank you for all the work you did on the comic. We had a pretty good run, didn't we?

YOU'RE WELCOME. SORRY I CAN'T HELP ANYMORE. I DO FEEL BAD ABOUT THAT.

No worries. We've both moved past all that now. Upward and onward, right?

I'M GLAD YOU FOUND A NEW ARTIST. HOPE THAT'S WORKING OUT FOR YOU.

Yeah, well, just between you and me, I think The Mighty Onion has run its course.

SERIOUSLY? WHAT DO YOU MEAN BY THAT?

Pam, I'm sure you'd agree that it's better to go out in a blaze of glory than to slowly fade away.

ARE YOU OK, ELIOT? YOU SOUND LIKE YOU'RE IN A WEIRD PLACE, EMOTIONALLY.

Actually, I feel GREAT right now. You know when you're having trouble deciding something, and then you finally decide? It's very liberating.

OK, I'M NOT SURE WHAT ALL THAT MEANS. BUT IT SOUNDS LIKE YOU KNOW WHAT YOU'RE DOING.

So how's everything going with Darn You Kids? Seems like you're having a lot of fun with it.

HA! APPEARANCES CAN BE DECEIVING, ELIOT.

SATURDAY

WELL, THE GOOD NEWS IS I FINALLY GOT A
LITTLE BIT AHEAD OF MY DEADLINES. IN FACT,
TODAY I WENT TO MELANIE'S HOUSE TO SEE IF SHE
COULD GO WITH ME TO THE BUBBLE TEA PLACE. HER
MOM SAID SHE WAS OUT SOMEWHERE WITH KAITLYN.
AND I DIDN'T SAY ANYTHING, BUT I WAS LIKE:

THAT CAN'T
BE RIGHT.

SHE'S NOT
FRIENDS WITH
KAITLYN.

SHE HATES
KAITLYN.

(FUNNY. AS I'M WRITING THIS, I'M LOOKING OUT MY
BEDROOM WINDOW AND I CAN SEE ELIOT DRAGGING
SOMETHING OUT OF HIS GARAGE. LOOKS LIKE ONE OF
THOSE METAL FIREPIT THINGS.)

ANYWAY, I ASKED HER TO TELL MELANIE TO CALL
ME WHEN SHE GETS HOME. BUT HERE IT IS, ALMOST
SUNDOWN, AND NO CALL OR TEXT OR ANYTHING.

(NOW ELIOT'S GOT A PRETTY BIG FIRE GOING. MAYBE HE'S MAKING S'MORES OR SOMETHING?)

SO I GOT TO THINKING ABOUT THAT LETTER MELANIE WROTE TO ME, AND THE THINGS I SAID WHEN I WROTE BACK TO HER. AND, I DON'T KNOW, AT THE TIME IT SEEMED SO OBVIOUS THAT I WAS RIGHT AND SHE WAS WRONG. BUT NOW I'M NOT SO SURE.

(NOW ELIOT'S SITTING NEXT TO THE FIREPIT WITH SOMETHING IN HIS LAP. HARD TO SEE WHAT IT IS. HE'S SUCH A WEIRD DUDE. LIKE THE OTHER DAY, WHEN HE WAS TALKING ABOUT "GOING OUT IN A BLAZE OF GLORY." NOW HERE HE IS IN HIS BACKYARD WITH A BIG OLD FIRE IN FRONT OF HIM, THROWING PIECES OF PA

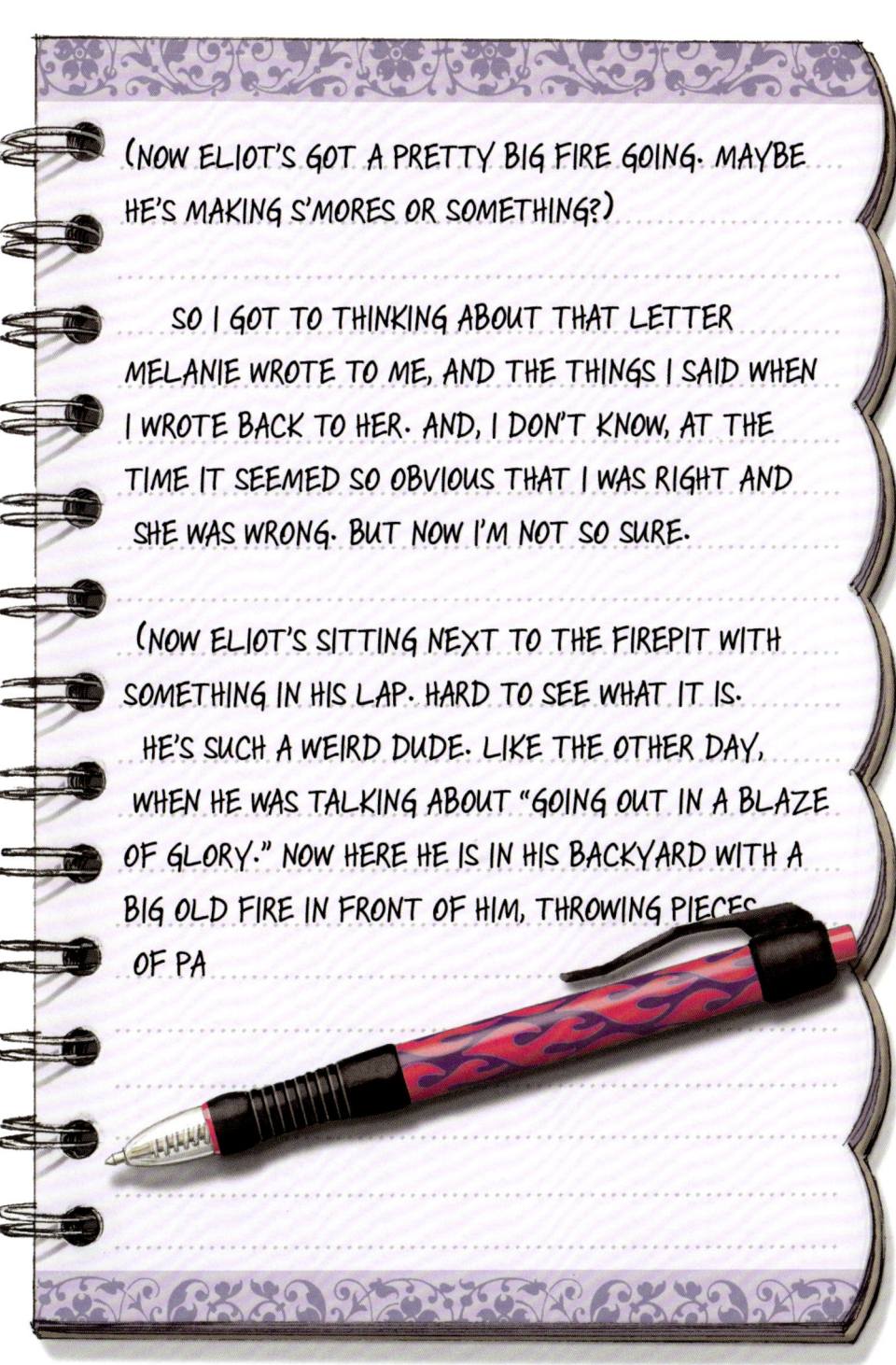

I'm still kind of processing how things went down last night. It was like something out of a movie. A really bizarre movie.

So, I had made this decision to set fire to every last page of The Mighty Onion. In retrospect, a choice I probably should have thought through a little more. But I swear it made sense to me at the time.

But I'd only burned one or two pages before I heard a girl's voice, screaming at me from a few houses away.

NEVER IN MY LIFE HAVE I YELLED SO LOUDLY.
I WAS SHOUTING, AND SPRINTING THROUGH PEOPLE'S
BACKYARDS, AND LEAPING OVER FENCES. IT WAS
PRETTY BONKERS.

PEOPLE MUST HAVE THOUGHT I'D LOST MY MIND.
BUT COME ON: THE DUDE WAS SETTING FIRE TO MY
COMIC! THERE WAS NO TIME FOR WORRYING ABOUT
MRS. LOMBARDI'S TULIP GARDEN.

Honestly, it looked as if Pam had been taken over by demonic forces or something. She cleared Mr. Polakowski's fence in a single bound, which is basically impossible. I tried that once a couple summers back, and ended up in the hospital.

By the time she got to my backyard, she was so angry I thought she was going to throw ME into the firepit.

I WAS ALL SET TO RIP INTO HIM, BUT THEN THIS
HUGE GUST OF WIND CAME ALONG AND SENT ALL
MY ORIGINAL ARTWORK FLYING UP INTO THE AIR.
SUDDENLY, THE ONLY THING THAT MATTERED WAS
RUNNING AFTER THOSE PAGES AND GRABBING THEM
BEFORE THEY GOT BLOWN INTO MRS. HURKLEMAN'S
SWIMMING POOL.

WE MANAGED TO GET EVERY PAGE BACK EXCEPT
ONE, WHICH SOMEHOW GOT SNAGGED AT THE TOP OF
A PINE TREE THAT WAS, LIKE, A HUNDRED FEET TALL.

So there I was, way up at the top of Mr. Gunderson's ponderosa pine, risking life and limb to get that last page. By leaning over and stretching as far as I could, I finally managed to get hold of it.

But then I lost my footing and basically bounced from branch to branch all the way down to the bottom of the tree, like some kind of rubbery cartoon character.

AND THAT'S HOW, INSTEAD OF SCREAMING AT ELIOT FOR TRYING TO BURN MY ARTWORK, I ENDED UP SITTING THERE PATCHING HIM UP WITH A WHOLE BOXFUL OF BANDAGES.

AND THEN, NO KIDDING: WE BOTH JUST STARTED LAUGHING. LIKE, BIG OLD BELLY LAUGHS. THE WHOLE SITUATION WAS JUST SO RIDICULOUS.

AND ELIOT APOLOGIZED, AND HE HAD TEARS IN HIS EYES, AND I TOLD HIM HE WAS AN UNBELIEVABLY INFURIATING PERSON. BUT THAT I CARED A LOT ABOUT OUR FRIENDSHIP AND THAT I MISSED WORKING WITH HIM. AND THOUGH I'D SAID THAT MAINLY JUST TO CHEER HIM UP, I REALIZED, AS SOON AS THE WORDS CAME OUT OF MY MOUTH, THAT IT WAS TRUE.

So Pam sat there, looking at her old Mighty Onion pages, and laughing at all the weird jokes and plot twists that barely make any sense. And suddenly she looked at me and said that working on Darn You Kids was no fun at all, and that she'd secretly gotten sick of it weeks ago.

And Lois was, like: "No skateboards. They're too modern."

Seriously? SKATEBOARDS?!

I mean, back in her day, that must have been cutting-edge technology.

When Pam got up to go home, she said she was taking all the pages back with her, which I agreed was for the best.

After she was gone, Mr. Gunderson came out and yelled at me for climbing his tree. And I just stood there with a big smile on my face.

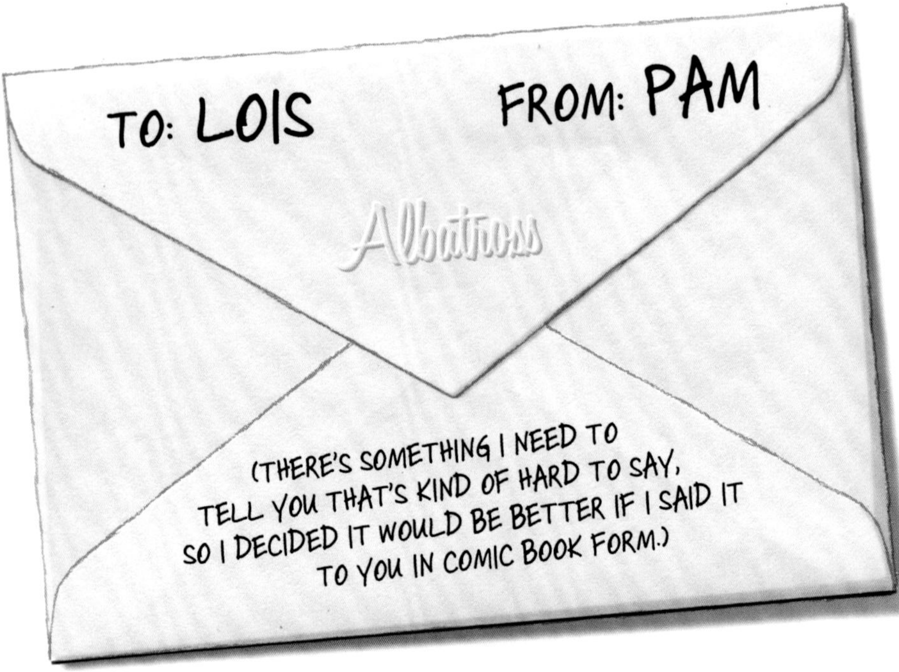
TO: LOIS
FROM: PAM
Albatross
(THERE'S SOMETHING I NEED TO TELL YOU THAT'S KIND OF HARD TO SAY, SO I DECIDED IT WOULD BE BETTER IF I SAID IT TO YOU IN COMIC BOOK FORM.)

SO, IN CASE IT ISN'T CLEAR, THE MAGICAL
SHOES ARE SYMBOLIC OF DARN YOU KIDS,
WALKING IS SYMBOLIC OF DRAWING, AND
PAM IS SYMBOLIC OF ME.

I TALKED TO MY MOM AND SHE SAID
TO DO THIS PROPERLY I NEED TO GIVE YOU
TWO WEEKS' NOTICE. SO I HOPE YOU CAN
FIND A NEW ARTIST IN TWO WEEKS.

THANK YOU FOR BELIEVING IN ME, LOIS.
I'M SORRY IF I'VE LET YOU DOWN.

BUT THERE'S NO GETTING AROUND IT:
I CAN'T WEAR THESE SHOES ANYMORE.

SINCERELY,

PAM

Letters to the Editor

To the editor,
I am writing to complain in the strongest
possible terms about the sudden cancellation
of *The Mighty Onion*. My granddaughter and
I w
ea ...this feature, and were
bu
e
p

Letters to the Editor

To the editor,
Would you ride a horse halfway across a
stream and then stop? Would you wear half a
hat? Would you ride a unicycle that has only
half a wheel? No, I don't think you would.

Then why in the blazes have you ceased
publication of *The Mighty Onion* when the
story is only half finished? As far as the readers know, the villain has escaped punishment
and the heroes have vanished into the fog!

Please reverse this decision. If you don't,
I'm not sure I can continue subscribing to
the *Bugle*.

> **Hubert Gruber**
> **Piffling**

To the editor,
Have you changed the ink you're using to
print the paper? It used to smell nice, but now
...paper has ever made.
Indeed, if anything should be canceled, it is the
dreadful *Darn You Kids*, which is about as funny
as an ingrown toenail.

> **Patty O' Firntcher**
> **East Blemish**

ed
n the
e read-
hment

MONDAY

I WAS WORRIED THAT LOIS WOULD BE SUPER ANGRY WITH ME FOR NOT WANTING TO DRAW DARN YOU KIDS ANYMORE. BUT TODAY, WHEN I HANDED IN THE LAST COUPLE WEEKS' WORTH OF STRIPS, SHE WAS SURPRISINGLY COOL ABOUT THE WHOLE THING.

AND SUDDENLY SHE ASKED ME IF I CAN TALK ELIOT INTO DOING ONE MORE ISSUE OF THE MIGHTY ONION! IF I KNOW HIM LIKE I THINK I DO, IT'S NOT LIKE I'M GONNA HAVE TO TWIST THE GUY'S ARM.

So Pam came up to me at school today and said Lois at the Piffling Bugle wants to run one more issue of The Mighty Onion!

I told her she needs to apologize to you, personally, for all the anguish and suffering she caused.

Also, no dice unless they run it in full color.

You said that?

SWEEET!!

Quick, let's think of more demands.

So here's my thinking. None of the Bugle readers ever saw that issue I did with Kitty. So we're gonna have to circle back and redo that whole part of the story. But here's the thing: This time, I've got the chance to have everything play out differently.

And I don't just mean getting rid of all the smiling flower stickers.

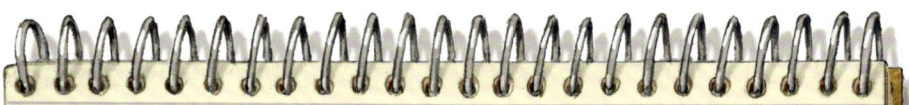

Of course, one little problem remained. Now I had to go up to Kitty and somehow find a nice way of telling her that I wouldn't be needing her services anymore because her drawings are terrible.

But before I could even open my mouth, she was like:

Sorry, Quiggler, but I can't draw The Mighty Onion anymore.

I'm creating a comic book of my own now, and...

...you know how it is...

...your work just doesn't speak to me the way it used to.

Oh no! I am completely devastated!

Every once in a while, things go my way. Like, once every ten years or something.

Pam, did you get a chance to read the new script? Sorry it's a little longer than usual.

ELIOT, YOU REALLY OUTDID YOURSELF. I MEAN, COME ON: 33 PAGES!

Yeah, I figured we needed to give readers something really big this time.

WELL, YOU DEFINITELY DID THAT. AND I LOVE THE SURPRISE APPEARANCE OF YOU-KNOW-WHO!

Thanks. I guess you'll have to come up with some kind of costume design for her, huh?

JUST YOU WAIT. I'VE ALREADY GOT SOME GOOD IDEAS FOR THAT.

What did you think of Guinea Pig Girl's superpower? I was afraid I went a little over the top with that.

SO GOOD. READERS ARE GONNA FLIP OUT WHEN THEY GET TO THAT PART.

Well, thanks in advance. This one is going to take up a lot of your time: the fight, the missile, all that stuff.

YEAH, BUT IT'LL BE WORTH IT. DON'T WANT TO JINX THINGS, BUT I THINK THIS COULD TURN OUT TO BE OUR BEST ISSUE YET!

THE CRAFTY KOALA!

DON'T ACT SO SURPRISED.

MIGRAINE AND I HAVE BEEN ALLIES FOR QUITE SOME TIME NOW.

YES. AND THAT IS A MISTAKE THAT YOU'RE GONNA START PAYING FOR...

KLANK!

KLANK!

KLANK!

WELL, WELL, WELL...

...IF IT ISN'T MY FAVORITE MEDDLESOME INTRUDER.

AND THIS TIME YOU'VE BROUGHT A FRIEND.

I TRUST YOU ENJOYED CATCHING UP WITH MY OLD CHUM, THE CRAFTY KOALA.

LIVES UP TO HER NAME, DOESN'T SHE?

WHATEVER IT IS YOU'RE PLANNING...

...YOU WON'T GET AWAY WITH IT!

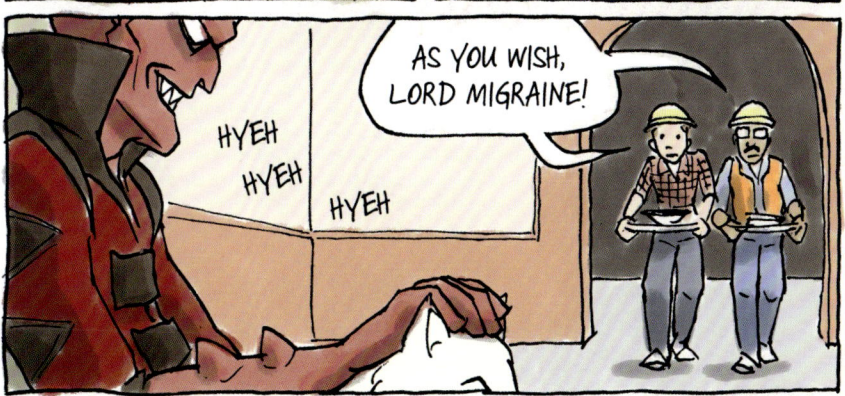

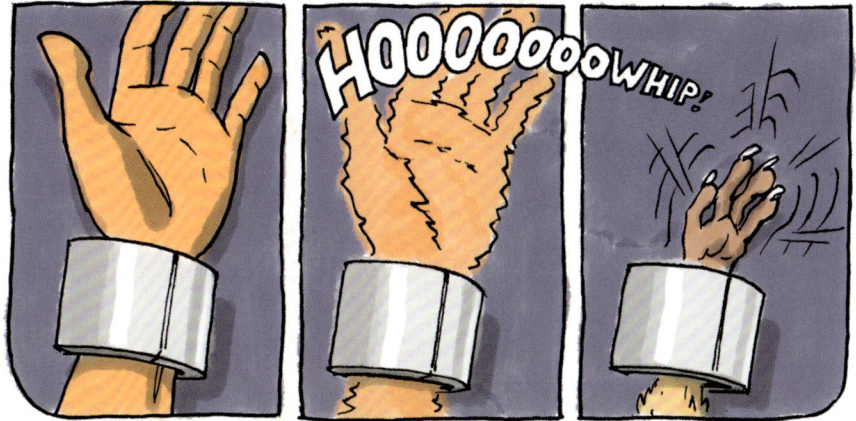

NOT GONNA LIE: IT'S KIND OF A DORKY SUPERPOWER.

BUT EVERY ONCE IN A WHILE IT COMES IN REAL HANDY.

TUP!

CHUP!

SHHHHHHHHHHH

WELL, THEN. LET'S GET THIS SHOW ON THE ROAD, SHALL WE?

HANK! OTIS!

INITIATE THE LAUNCH!

AS YOU WISH, LORD MIGRAINE!

10...

...9...

KRASH!

...8...

WHAT THE...?

SEVERAL DAYS LATER, AFTER CAPTAIN MIGRAINE AND THE CRAFTY KOALA HAVE BEEN CARTED OFF TO JAIL, COMMISSIONER GROBAN HOLDS A SPECIAL CEREMONY IN HONOR OF OUR FEARLESS HEROES.

...BUT BEFORE WE BRING THE EVENING TO A CLOSE, I HAVE A SPECIAL SURPRISE TO UNVEIL.

OK, FRED. THROW THE SWITCH!

BVVVVVV

AFTER THE CEREMONY, GUINEA PIG GIRL SAYS SHE NEEDS TO TELL THE MIGHTY ONION ABOUT AN IMPORTANT DECISION SHE'S MADE.

WOW, ARE YOU SURE ABOUT THIS, GUINNY?

JOINING THE JUSTICE COMMITTEE MEANT SO MUCH TO YOU!

YEAH, BUT I'VE GOTTA STEP DOWN.

THE PAPERWORK IS A NIGHTMARE.

AND DON'T EVEN GET ME STARTED ON THE SOCIALIZING.

SERIOUSLY: I HAVE TO DO STUFF WITH THEM EVERY OTHER WEEKEND. IT'S EXHAUSTING!

SAY, HAVE YOU EVER BEEN TO PEPE'S PIZZA PALACE?

NO. WHY?

IT'S ONLY A COUPLE BLOCKS FROM HERE, AND THEY'RE OPEN LATE.

C'MON, LET'S GO GRAB A SLICE!

YOUR TREAT?

OF COURSE!

SO, HOW DID YOU BECOME GUINEA PIG GIRL, ANYWAY?

DID YOU GET BITTEN BY A RADIOACTIVE GUINEA PIG?

JUSTIN, PLEASE.

Letters to the Editor

BUGL

To the editor,
What a pleasure it was to see that you
decided to bring back *The Mighty Onion*.
And you sure did pull out all the stops, didn't
~~~ seeing anything in the

E PIFFLIN

yo
ea
bu
e
p

Letters to the Editor

To the editor,
I am writing to commend Eliot Quigly
and Pamela Jones for their outstanding work
on your special full-color edition of *The
Mighty Onion* this past weekend. I think it's
fair to say it's among the best things the *Bugle*
has ever done. When I got to the end of it, I
went right back and started reading again from
the beginning.
Don't tell me this is the last we'll see of
this feature. I'm sure I speak for many when
I say, "Long live *The Mighty Onion!*"

sed
n the
e read-
hment

BUG

Sean Zaileezay
Piffling

To the editor,
I hate to be "that guy," but your recent opinion
piece on the da~~~ rs of using dental floss to repair
~~~ nope that you'll consider running more
issues of it. Because I can't remember the last
time I had such fun reading the *Bugle*!

Lou Scannon
Blemish

Dear Eliot and Pam,

This was by far the best issue you've

thrillin
so clev
azing!

Migrain
nspired
utstandin
rilliment

GERO GELUPPI

nk goodness you two
ether again, because
the best comics I've
d more exciting, until
nd up and cheer!

e you'll ke
c, since w
d more of
ntures!

r fan
forever,

ourtney

Dear Eliot and Pam,

Man, oh man, the latest
absolutely incredible!
As you know, I like to
overusing the word "grea
in the case of The Mighty
"great" is the only word
really fits! The story and
mind-blowing, and I lo
he Crafty Koala, and he

2 WORDS: MORE, PLEASE!

om the Desk of
ie Wellingto

Dearest Elliot and Pamela,

Never for a second did I doubt that a return t
form was well within your capabilities, but ther
is little that could have prepared me for the
verve and inventive prowess that was on display
in the latest issue of The Mighty Onion.

As I turned from one sumptuous page to the
next, I was put in mind of the words of Marcel
Proust, who once penned these immortal lines:
"_le véritable voyage de découverte ne consiste_

Dear

What
whole
great
kept s

HI, MELANIE. CAN WE TALK? I REALLY NEED TO APOLOGIZE TO YOU.

Yeah, maybe we both need to do that. I feel awful about that letter I wrote. For real.

NOT AS MUCH AS I REGRET SCREWING UP OUR FRIENDSHIP SO BADLY.

Hey, a big opportunity came your way and you went for it. I should have been cheering you on.

YEAH, WELL, THAT BIG OPPORTUNITY DIDN'T TURN OUT TO BE SO MUCH FUN.

Seriously? What went wrong with it?

KIND OF A LONG STORY.
I'LL TELL YOU ABOUT IT
NEXT TIME WE HANG OUT.

So when are you free?
After school today
would work for me.

TODAY'S PERFECT.
HOW ABOUT THE BUBBLE
TEA PLACE? MY TREAT!

Hey, I'm not gonna
say no to that! But
will the owner treat
us like hoodlums?

IF SHE DOES, WE CAN
LEAVE AND GO SOMEWHERE
ELSE. THERE'S ALWAYS
THE SQUISHY BURGER.

Ooh, let's just
go there instead.
Their onion rings
are the BEST!

ON TUESDAY, MELANIE AND I GOT TOGETHER AFTER SCHOOL. WE WERE GONNA GO TO SQUISHY BURGER, BUT IN THE END WE JUST HEADED OVER TO THE GURGLING MEADOWS ELEMENTARY PLAYGROUND AND PUSHED EACH OTHER ON THE SWINGS.

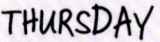

REMEMBER THAT HALLOWEEN WHEN YOU DRESSED UP AS THE RED TELETUBBY?

COME ON, PAM, GET THE STORY STRAIGHT. HE'S PURPLE, AND HE HAS A NAME.

TINKY-WINKY!

IT WAS GREAT SEEING HER AGAIN AFTER SO MANY WEEKS. I WAS AFRAID THERE MIGHT BE SOME AWKWARD-NESS, BUT IT WAS JUST LIKE OLD TIMES: MAKING WEIRD JOKES AND LAUGHING SO LOUDLY THAT MOTHERS WOULDN'T LET THEIR KIDS COME NEAR US.

THEN YESTERDAY, GLADYS SMYLIE TOOK ME
AND MY MOM OUT FOR DINNER AT THIS UPSCALE
RESTAURANT SHE LOVES TO GO TO, MOOO-LIN ROUGE.
SHE WANTED TO THANK ME FOR ALL THE ARTWORK I
DID, WHICH SHE SAID WAS JUST PERFECT.

HALFWAY THROUGH THE MEAL, SHE LET US IN ON
A LITTLE SECRET: SHE'S DECIDED TO COME OUT OF
RETIREMENT AND DO ONE LAST YEAR OF DARN YOU
KIDS, BEFORE ENDING IT FOR GOOD.

LOOK, I'LL LEVEL
WITH YOU: MY JOKES
HAVEN'T BEEN FUNNY
IN DECADES.

BUT THE STUFF
LOIS WAS COMING
UP WITH?

GOOD GRIEF!

WE'RE LUCKY GLADYS INSISTED ON PAYING THE
BILL, BECAUSE I'VE NEVER SEEN PRICES LIKE THAT IN
MY ENTIRE LIFE.

Mooo-Lin Rouge

Great Food
Fine Wines
Dim Lighting

Starters

HERB-ENCRUSTED HERBS 28

STEAMED POPCORN 27

SLOW-ROASTED JELLYFISH 38

BOWL OF UNSALTED PRETZELS 28
ADD MUSTARD 38

Soup

ROOM-TEMPERATURE GOULASH 33

CHILLED PARSLEY WATER 27

Entrees

BLACKENED FILET OF GROUND CHUCK 88

POULET FRIT DU KENTUCKY 75

PAN-FRIED DAFFODIL STEMS 78

CREAMED ANCHOVIES IN A PILE 68

BRAISED NEW ENGLAND PIER BARNACLES Market Price

Desserts

MELTED SCOOP OF ROCKY ROAD 39

DUSTING OF POWDERED SUGAR ON A PLATE 48

COOKIE 53

70% Gratuity on Parties of 4 or More

So I got to thinking about Jack Baccarat's advice on quitting while you're ahead or whatever, and it suddenly hit me: Just because a dude gets to be the big cheese at a comic company doesn't mean he's not a complete doofus. Or maybe I misinterpreted what he was saying. I prefer the first explanation.

Anyway, I went down the street to this "free library" thing and stuck Jack's book in there. Because if I had quit when he told me to, I would've missed the chance to do the best writing of my entire life.

The Shining.

I wonder what this one is about.

On the way home I stopped at Squishy Burger for lunch, and I remembered how Pam and I wrote the "New Rules" on a bunch of napkins. And while I was sitting there, I thought about how close I came to total catastrophe with the firepit and the box of matches and all that.

So I decided to make some more rules: this time just personal ones that would apply only to me.

Excuse me, could I get a felt-tip pen?

Sir, look at the menu. That's all we got.

Luckily, I was able to borrow one from another customer.

ELIOT'S RULES

RULE #1 : Never destroy Pam's artwork. It's wrong, and also when she finds out about it, she will grab you by the neck and body slam you.

RULE #2: Don't make big life decisions based only on advice you got from a fortune cookie.

RULE #3: When you've built the entire series around two main characters, it's maybe not such a great idea to have one of them get hurled off the side of a cliff.

RULE #4: Don't be envious of people. (Basically impossible, but at least TRY.)

I hereby agree to all these rules!

Eliot

TODAY AT SCHOOL, MRS. MACONIE CAME OVER AND SAID SHE WAS SORRY ABOUT EVERYTHING I WENT THROUGH WITH DARN YOU KIDS AND ALL THE DEAD-LINES AND EVERYTHING. I TOLD HER THERE WAS NO NEED TO APOLOGIZE, BECAUSE IT WAS A GREAT LEARNING EXPERIENCE FOR ME.

THEN SHE SAID SHE HAD SOMETHING SPECIAL FOR ME. I GUESS HER NIECE IS A SECOND GRADE TEACHER AT GURGLING MEADOWS ELEMENTARY, AND EVERY DAY THEY HAVE STORYBOOK TIME, WHEN SHE READS TO THE KIDS. BUT THEN ONE DAY INSTEAD OF A PICTURE BOOK, SHE READ SOME MIGHTY ONION ISSUES TO THEM.

...AND THEN ONE OF THE KIDS SAT DOWN WITH HER CRAYONS AND MADE THIS FOR YOU.

ISN'T THAT JUST THE SWEETEST?

Dear Pam,

I love your drawings. You are a big inspirashun to me. When I grow up I want to be a comic book artist just like you.

from
Clare

LOOKING AT THAT LETTER MADE ME GET KIND OF
EMOTIONAL. WHEN I STARTED DRAWING THE MIGHTY
ONION, I NEVER IMAGINED THAT MY WORK COULD BE
AN INSPIRATION TO ANYONE, LET ALONE A LITTLE KID.
SUDDENLY, I WAS FILLED WITH ENERGY TO KEEP GOING,
TO MAKE MORE AND MORE COMICS WITH ELIOT FOR AS
LONG AS HE WANTED TO KEEP WRITING THEM.

I GUESS IN THE END EVERYTHING WORKED OUT
THE WAY IT NEEDED TO. SURE, IT WAS EXCITING TO
BE ON A RADIO SHOW AND TO HAVE PEOPLE TAKING
PHOTOS OF ME. BUT IF THE ONLY WAY TO GET THAT
STUFF IS TO WORK ON A PROJECT THAT I KIND OF
SECRETLY HATE, I'M BETTER OFF STICKING WITH
SOMETHING THAT MAKES ME HAPPY.

LIKE DRAWING PICTURES OF A GUINEA PIG
WEARING A CAPE. THAT MAKES ME HAPPY.

REALLY HAPPY.

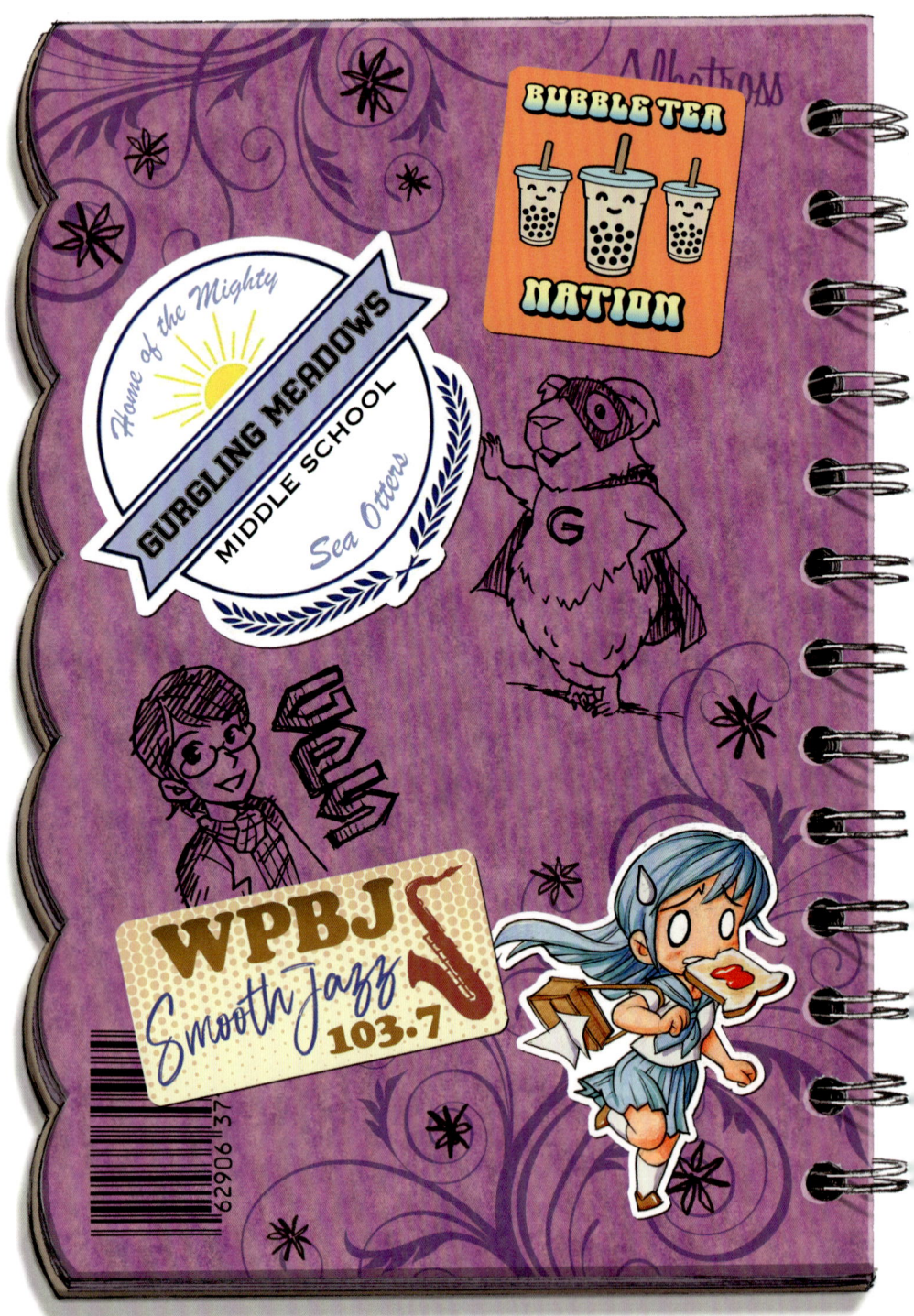

THE MAKING OF
THE MIGHTY
ONION

THE ORAJIN of
ONION RING MAN
SUPEREST HERO OF THEM ALL!!

When I first came up with the idea for this series, I thought the name of Eliot's superhero might be Onion Ring Man. Giving it a little more thought, I decided that was too on the nose, even by Eliot's standards!

THE LIGHT'S TURNING RED.

I'D BETTER COME TO A FULL AND COMPLETE STOP.

WHEN SUDDENLY...

Foooooo

WHAT THE...

FWAP

In an early version of the story, the Mighty Onion was a fully grown adult in real life. Here, you see him wearing a necktie and driving a car. When I later chose to make him a lot younger, that meant changing his clothing and having him ride a bicycle instead.